MUSE-DREAM
MYSTERIES

S.R. LONGSHORE'S

MUSE-DREAM MYSTERIES

Ordering Information:

BookTrail Agency
8838 Sleepy Hollow Rd.
Kansas City, MO 64114

Printed in the United States of America

Contents

DEDICATION

I am dedicating my stories to the following people:

Touch Not – to my mother, Doris Baine Taylor Batten.
She used to tell me to be careful about the people
I get involved with and the things I choose to do.

Her Name is Anoi – to my grandfather, William Lee
Samuel Taylor. He was a prayer warrior who fought
hard for his family and what he believed in.

And With a Flash – to my grandmother, Maggie
White Taylor. She always used to say that the choices
I make now will determine my outcome later.

The Gift – to my aunt who raised me, Vernice Pecolia
Taylor Reynolds. She died young but was an extremely
loving and patient person. She endured a lot of hardship
but she was always positive and encouraging.

The Trip – to my aunt who loved my stories and
encouraged me to write, Della Marian Taylor Hubbard.

I wouldn't have chosen any other people to be
my relatives. I loved each of them dearly.

TOUCH NOT

Many years ago, far, far away, there was a small village centered in the most beautiful and serene forest. The forest provided everything that the villagers needed for an enchanted life. Once a week, they would all come together to celebrate their appreciation by giving praises to what they called the "Great Spirit." They would dance and sing songs to It. Songs that told tales of adventure and mystery. They also told stories which had been passed down for generations. Stories of Its protection and Its wrath. And each night before they went to sleep, they would bow in their dwellings to thank It. They felt that if they did not thank It, their land and life would be cursed. This is why they believed that they lived peacefully among the animals. And no one ever came to attack them. Also their vegetation grew in abundance. Harvesting was easy. Fruit would fall from the trees sweet and juicy, with no rottenness at all. Plants would easily spring from the ground with little effort in replanting them. The weather was never too hot or cold. Soft rains would fall to keep everything fresh and watered. They had springs for bathing and drinking.

Things couldn't be more perfect in their eyes. However, as happy and thankful as they seemed, not all of them had the same mindset.

There was a local spirit healer named Tertsrick. He was very jealous of the Great Spirit. He wanted to be worshiped and live forever like It did. The spirit healers were blessed with substantially longer life, but no one lived forever. Since the villagers rarely needed medical attention beyond an occasional bite or break, the local spirit healer was mainly there to provide daily blessings and prayers to the Great Spirit for the people. Then he was to in turn bless the people with the words from the Great Spirit, for only the spirit healer could hear directly from It.

Now Tertsrick was getting old and feared that his days would soon be over because the Great Spirit had shown him his successor. During those days, a young man was always chosen and the present spirit healer must teach him all that he knows. Once a successor was chosen, the Great Spirit would impart the blessing of long life upon him. Later, when the present spirit healer's days were over, he would go away beyond the hills to the "Resting Place." This was a holy place where all the spirit healers rested in eternity. This place was secret, and no one but the spirit healers could go there. It was not even revealed to them until it was their time to move on.

But Tertsrick was stubborn and would not go to the young man. So he devised a plan that he thought would allow him to live longer, possibly forever. Instead of acknowledging his successor, Tertsrick told the people that the Great Spirit was not pleased with them because someone among them was insincere. He said that the Great Spirit had shown him who it was and that a human sacrifice would be required. The people wondered what happened to anger It. But they didn't question Tertsrick because they had such great respect for him.

Tertsrick pointed to the father of the young man who was supposed to be his successor. He said that the man and his family had to be punished for among them was much sin. He then pointed to the son and said that he had to be sacrificed as a warning to others. Tertsrick also said that more sacrifices would be necessary if the people did not believe.

Human sacrifices were rare. So whatever caused the Great Spirit to require this from the family must have been something horrible. The father of the boy held his son and cried out, "No, my son nor my family has done anything to deserve this."

But Tertsrick demanded, and the people in fear of the Great Spirit pulled the young man from his father. The father fell to his knees and wept along with his other family members. "Why?" he cried. "If the Great Spirit is so great and angry with us then why hasn't It spoken to me, for I am responsible for what my family does? And why sacrifice my son instead of me?"

"Silence," some yelled, "before a worse thing come upon you and yours."

Tertsrick took his successor and murdered him. He drank his blood because it contained the blessing of long life. And once he began to age again, he planned on drinking the blood of the next chosen one. Tertsrick smirked and laid down to sleep with a wide conniving grin for he thought he had outsmarted everyone, even the Great Spirit. Now he did not know just how right he was, and yet, oh so wrong. The Great Spirit is a permissive spirit. It will let you do some of the things you desire. However, for every heinous act performed an even greater recompense is required.

This act angered the Great Spirit and It visited Tertsrick in his hut. The hut turned cold, and abnormally dark. Then a reddish-gray mist filled the dwelling. The form of a hand appeared from the mist and grabbed Tertsrick by the throat. It threw him to the floor with great force. An enormous bright light fixed upon him and in a thunderous voice that only Tertsrick could hear, It demanded him to lay with his face towards the ground. It spoke with such power that Tertsrick's skin fluttered like a kite in the wind.

It yelled, "Tertsrick, I cannot be tricked. Since you do not want to die, then you will not." A streak of lightening flashed and struck Tertsrick in his right eye, blinding it. At the same time, it turned him into a translucent liquid and said that the first thing he fell upon is what he would become. He would have to live like that thing forever. The thing that he touched would also live forever, and together, the two would be cursed.

After It spoke, Tertsrick ran into the forest hoping to escape. Panting with fear, he tripped upon an odd-looking stump that was attached to a fully-grown tree. When he tripped, he fell and embraced the tree to catch himself. And because he touched the tree, he and the tree became one and the two became calcified, but they did not die.

The tree could feel Tertsrick as he absorbed into its rings, bark, roots, and all its parts. It didn't like that Tertsrick had become a part of it, so it moaned and groaned. Once Tertsrick was fully absorbed, the tree let out a high-pitched screech that caused the animals to stop and freeze from fear. Only they could hear it. Because Tertsrick drank blood, he caused the tree to turn a beautiful deep glossy red. Darker streaks of blood formed swirly patterns along the trunk and branches. It was a strange sight, but in many ways, more beautiful than all the other trees of the forest.

Now the people grieved over the boy's life. Nevertheless, they gathered to sing praises in fear of further upsetting the Great Spirit. They hoped that no more sacrifices would be required. Before when the Great Spirit spoke, a rumbling noise would fill the sky, shaking their huts and cause them to quiver. This time when the people heard the thunder only coming from Tertsrick's dwelling, they knew something was wrong and that it was a sign that the Great Spirit was upset. Many speculated that Tertsrick had not told them something, and the Spirit was demanding Its voice to be heard. Especially since It had only disturbed Tertsrick's hut. The people waited anxiously outside to hear what the Spirit had to say. Unknowingly to them, Tertsrick had fled into the forest.

But as they waited, they heard loud moaning coming from the woods and the ground began to vibrate. In fear, they ran to the river and waded in the water. They knew something was wrong and hoped that whatever was causing the commotion would not come after them. If it did, they would have a head start and try to swim away. But after a while, everything became quiet. They decided to return to the village, and when they did, everything seemed normal except for a strange figure floating in the air. Even though they were afraid, they believed it had something to do with the Great Spirit, so they bowed and began to worship.

Now, when Tertsrick blended with the tree, a mist in the shape of a ball moved to the center of the village. This is what the people saw when they returned home. From it, the Great Spirit spoke to the people and said, "Fear not, for I am the Great Spirit that you worship, and I am not angry with you. Tertsrick deceived you and committed a horrible act. The young man he sacrificed was his successor. Tertsrick became jealous and killed him. I have punished him for that. He wanted to live eternally, so now he does. Since Tertsrick was evil, I will no longer trust only one person to relay my words. I will now speak directly to you so no one else will be able to trick you. I may also tell another so you will be convinced of what I am saying."

"Therefore, you must continue to do good and worship me as before. If you do, I will continue to take care of you. If you do not, evil will happen to you as well. But you must leave this place. I will show you another place. For this place is now evil because of what Tertsrick has done."

So, the people moved on and never returned. As time went on, stories were told, but the place was never revisited. Generations have passed and the place has been forgotten. Many are not even sure if the stories are true. To be truthful, no one seems to care. Over time, the people grew great, and they each took their closest kin and spread out.

∽

Much later, and early one Saturday morning, a youngster named Donovan wakes up excited. Today, he and eleven other children who live in an orphanage are going to the museum. Escorting them are two House Mothers. At all times, the Mothers are responsible for making sure the children are properly cared for and protected. There are also Guardian Fathers who maintain the orphanage's upkeep. One of the Fathers will be driving the bus to the museum.

Together, the Mothers and Fathers share the educational and disciplinary responsibilities. The top overseers are a Superior Mother and a Primary Father. They make sure everything runs efficiently and provide guidance to the staff and the children.

The orphanage is small and located in a quaint hillside village about ten miles from town. The town is more like a metropolis. It's modernized where some of the villages seem almost antiquated. This is because the villages try to maintain simplicity. People feel that keeping things pure and simple make for a cleaner and healthier environment. But they do have electricity and plumbing.

There are rarely more than twelve children at an orphanage at one time. Children come here when there has been a great tragedy and no one else can care for an extra child. In this part of the world, there are ten villages, each with their own orphanage. Together, they form a perfect circumference around the town.

The town is where the museum is located. Most people live in the villages. The people who live in town are wealthy business and factory owners or people who work for one of the owners. The villagers are mostly farmers, craftsmen, teachers or local store and restaurant owners. And most of their businesses are family-owned and run. Usually, the villagers' main reason for coming into town is to bring a fresh supply of food items and merchandise, such as furniture and clothing that are still made the original way. But the town is also a great place to see new things and people they have not seen in a while.

Donovan's orphanage makes it their business to visit the town at least once a year to sell items the children made. Most of the money is used to help with expenses but a little is divided among the children. This is one of the ways the children are taught the importance of earning their keep. Sometimes, the visits are for fun. Today is one of those days.

The museum holds artifacts of the villages' history. It is the largest building in town and its main attraction. The last time Donovan's orphanage visited the museum, he was too ill to go. He had not been there long and the Mothers felt his illness was due to sadness, so they decided to let him stay home and rest. Because of that, Donovan only heard stories about the artifacts, and he was especially intrigued with one of them, a door.

The Door is kept in a protected environment. The story is that the Door belonged to a famous banker who disappeared after being revealed as a thief. When the people could not find the banker, they removed as many items as possible to replace the money that had been stolen. What they did not take, they burned, except for the huge entrance door and its frame. It was too beautiful with its red stain and iridescent sparkles. It had to be expensive, they thought. So the people decided to place it in the museum as a part of the town's history. It would serve as a reminder of how something so beautiful could be attached to something so ugly. And, hauntingly, it is said that the Door never looks quite the same twice. Most people believe that this part of the story is just for fun because the Door always looked the same to them. This made Donovan even more curious. He had to see for himself if the Door would change.

After hearing the stories about the Door, Donovan would have a recurring dream. It would always begin with him standing outside of the museum, waiting in line to get a ticket. Each ticket had a number which appeared on a car seat. The seats were connected like on a rollercoaster. The people didn't walk around the museum; they rode through it on a track. Donovan looked at his ticket; it was number one. This meant he had to sit at the front.

Once in the car, Donovan had to place headphones on to hear the guide speaking. The tour guide sat at the back and spoke through a microphone.

One by one, everyone loaded in. Donovan watched the people boarding, and they all seemed strange. He also noticed that those who came out of the museum had funny looks on their faces, somewhat like zombies or robots. This made him nervous, but it did not stop him from wanting to see what was inside.

As the ride began to move, the guide explained that the tour would take them from the towns' beginning events and end with the most recent. To reach each new level, the cars elevated circularly. This was fun for Donovan. He was so excited; he could hardly contain himself. But when he looked back at the other riders, they were emotionless. No one was talking, just turning their heads from side to side. Though this too was peculiar, he decided not to focus on them and just enjoy the ride.

When the cars reached the top level, there was a large dark hole, oblong-shaped. Each car amazingly individually elevated and moved forward into the hole. Inside, Donovan could see men in missile-like aircraft as well as hear them talking. This hole was a launching pad. However looking at all the small blinking lights inside made it seem as though the aircraft were in space. Donovan knew that this was the end of the tour because he had seen everything from stone wheels to rockets. But still, the cars began to go up farther, up to the roof.

Once the cars reached the roof, other people were sitting around the edge. They were motionless, not like in a daze but as though they were scared stiff. Then the ride came to a stop. Donovan's door opened, and he was ejected. He rolled to the ground, stood as quickly as possible and looked at the ride. He was puzzled. Why did that just happen and why did it only happen to him, he thought. All the other riders were still inside. They had the same frightened look on their faces as those sitting on the ledge. Donovan thought that maybe an exhibition was about to occur, and he was the first to participate. But when the ride slowly backed up until it completely disappeared, he knew that couldn't be it.

Brushing himself off, Donovan went to the side of the roof and sat. He was glad that it had a railing for they were up extremely high. He tried questioning some of the others, but no one said anything. He looked around and could not see an immediate way down. As he looked over the railing, he noticed something odd. It seemed as though they were sitting on a large, steep, grassy hill. No one would have known that there was a building underneath. And far down at the bottom of the hill was the street mall full of people walking around, totally unaware that they were up there.

Suddenly, a horn sounded. It blew three times and was chilling each time it blew. Donovan wondered even more why they were up there and why was he chosen out of all the others riders? He just couldn't figure it out.

He could hear dogs barking like they were chasing something. Soon a heavyset, dark-haired, somewhat grungy man came from the back running. He ran as fast as he could, leaped over the rail, fell and rolled. But he was able to get up and keep running.

The people on the side started moving their legs up and down as though they were running. Some were trembling and some were sweating, but all were in serious panic mode. Donovan decided to follow the man who jumped and run as fast as he could. He didn't know what was about to happen, and he didn't want to wait to find out.

The man ran in one direction and Donovan ran in another. Now he could hear men yelling, "Stop them!" A lot of bumbling noise and people screaming came from the top, but Donovan didn't look back. He was too frightened, and he used his fear to propel him even faster. He did look somewhat to his right side, and he could see the other man still running. He could tell he was possibly getting tired because he began to lose his footing. He felt sorry for him, but he thought whatever was chasing them, it would get the slowest person first.

Donovan made it all the way to the unaware crowd. He desperately tried to blend in, hoping that he would go unnoticed or that whatever was chasing him would stop since he was in public view. He hid behind a newsstand, acting as if he wanted to buy a paper. But he was actually checking out the crowd to see if anyone had followed him.

He was extremely nervous and didn't know what to do next. Should he tell someone, and would they believe him? Should he go home, or would someone be there waiting for him? The percept of his thoughts was so overwhelming that he would always wake up sweating and panting at this part of the dream. He had no idea what it meant or why he frequently dreamed of it.

Another reason Donovan was so interested in visiting the museum was that he never knew how he arrived at the orphanage. He was told the museum contained all kinds of history and records. Maybe, just maybe, it would help him find out where he came from. Most of the children knew what caused them to be there. He knew that his last name was Reesa. But no one could ever give him any other information. Some said this and some said that but nothing exact. Once, he approached the Primary Father with the question, and he encouraged him not to worry. It didn't really matter, he explained, because it wouldn't change anything. He said that if the records were not clear, there was a reason. And sometimes somethings are better left unknown. So, this is what Donovan did, even though it hurt not knowing. However, he kept it in the back of his mind that if he would ever visit the museum, he would try to find out. He would make it a day to get answers about himself and the Door. But the Door would have to come first. He knew he could go on without knowing the truth of his past. But he had to know what was up with that door.

But there was a problem. Donovan was told that when visiting the museum, he would only have a few minutes at each place since there is so much to see. This was not good enough for him. He had to have more time to investigate, so he came up with a plan that when the House Mothers would make the children move on, he would hide and go back to discover as much as he could about the Door.

~

After a nice hearty breakfast, everyone boarded the bus. Slowly, it began to carry the children to their destination. The bus driver, a Guardian Father, had to be careful. Some of the roads were narrow and had not been paved. This made the bus rock quite often. And driving down the mountains were not easy. Therefore, extreme caution was always a priority. Even Donovan occasionally gripped the bottom of his seat.

When the town was in sight, Donovan's heart began to race. Though at a distance, he could tell that it was very different from the countryside. He could see one building that was clearly taller than the rest. This had to be the museum, he thought. It had a huge diamond-shaped sphere projecting from the roof, flickering vibrant colors as the sun gleamed on it. Oh, what a beautiful sight it must be to stand at the top and look out of it, he imagined. He just knew that he would be able to see the entire town from there. What delight he felt.

As the bus drew closer, Donovan could see that the roof looked more like a giant glass bell and the diamond-shaped sphere was the handle someone would use to ring the bell. Or maybe it looked more like the top of a candy dish which he could take off and see all the wonders inside. Now, the colors didn't just flicker. They burst out in rays of blue, green, yellow, and red. This reminded him of what he heard about the Door and its array of colors.

The closer the bus inched, the more excited Donovan became. He would hold his breath so often that he had to remind himself to breathe. To him, it was as though the bus would never get there. It was as if it was moving slower and slower. That was because the closer it got to the town, the heavier the traffic became. But he knew it wouldn't be long now that all the streets were paved. The smooth roads allowed the bus to move easier.

Once the bus entered the town's limits, bicycles, cars and walkers were scurrying all about. Vendors selling everything from food to clothing to crafts lined the streets. Musicians were playing, people miming and dancers performing, all hoping to accrue a few dollars. What a sight to see Donovan, said to himself. He, too, wanted to do something exciting, something great. He did not know what, but he secretly believed the Door could be the key. He wasn't sure why. Maybe because of the mystery surrounding it. He thought if he could solve the mystery, he would be famous. People everywhere would say, "Ask Donovan. He knows all there is to know about the Door." As he thought, he smiled and whispered, "Yes, that's exactly what I'm going to do."

Finally, the bus pulled up to the museum entrance. Now he understood what the beams of colors were. They were colors projecting from cuts of colored glass. Actual stained pictures within the glass. Pictures of important town historical events and famous people. In the front of the museum leading to the inside was a huge revolving door. On each side of the revolving door were automatic double doors. This was all so amazing to Donovan because the village's buildings were simple. And the tallest structures were the factories and mills.

As the bus was coming to a stop, one of the House Mothers got up to speak. She explained all the rules that had to be followed and what time the bus would be leaving so everyone would be back to the bus on time. She said that everyone would be divided into two groups and stressed the importance of staying together. By the time she finished speaking, a museum official came to the door.

When he got on, he went over all the ins and outs of the museum and what to do just in case someone needed help. He gave each one a visitor's pass, a map of the museum that highlighted some of the major attractions, and a ticket for one free meal. After all the instructions, everyone was divided into groups, red and blue, with one House Mother to each group.

The children were allowed to choose which group they wanted to be in. The blue group was to enter first, and most of them tried to enter that group. But not Donovan. He purposely wanted to be in the red group and at the end of the line. He thought that would give him a better chance to slip away. But he didn't realize that this lineup was only for how they would enter the building and not how the tour would take place. There was much more to discuss before the actual tour began.

One of the House Mothers asked Donovan if he was okay because he did not rush to get into the line. She knew how excited he was to go on the trip. Donovan looked up and smiled as he nodded that he was okay. The Guardian Father encouraged her not to worry. He believed that Donovan was a good boy, and he was just being polite. He said that Donovan is maturing and knew that there was no need to push or shove. He knew that everyone would eventually get in. "Ain't that right, Don," he asked. This time, Donovan replied with a "Yes, sir" and a salute. They all giggled and proceeded to get off the bus.

As they lined up to go inside, something so amazing caught Donovan's eye. It was a picture of the Door, stained right into one of the entrance doors. Wow, he thought! This Door must be pretty amazing since they would show a picture of it on the outside. But why? he wondered. "There has to be much more about the Door than what I was told," he mumbled. Now he was for certain that he had to get to that Door.

～

Once inside, the museum is designed to take visitors from the present to the past so that they would have a back-in-time experience. In the center, there is a stairway that leads to each level if someone desired to walk up. Many people like to use it for taking pictures. But as far as seeing the sights, most people take the elevator.

Also, there is a moving sidewalk on each floor that will allow visitors to view the artifacts. It is slow, but it is good for people who have difficulties. However, Donovan was certain that they would be walking because that would take too long. Their time was limited. And that made him happy because he believed that walking would allow him to easily blend in with the crowd, then slip away without being noticed.

From what Donovan could see, the museum was far more amazing than he had imagined. Replicas of birds and planes were hanging from the ceiling, moving back and forth as though they were flying on their own. He stared so hard that a man, who ended up being one of the tour guides, noticed. He said, "If you like these, wait until you see the floor with the life-size sea animals. Some of them are replicas, but most are original bones. It's going to be awesome to see how huge they are. People like to pose next to them for pictures. The animals are so enormous that people look like mice next to elephants. On another floor, there are mummies encased in glass. Some will be partially bandaged, but some look just like they are sleeping. They will be on the floor with the reenactment of death and torture techniques. That can be pretty spooky stuff, kid."

Donovan, with his eyes wide opened, nodded.

"You betcha," the man said as he continued to talk. "Oh, there are all kinds of good stuff like the floor with the battle artillery and war gear. All the floors will have waxed people from that era. They will look so real that their eyes seem to follow you. Some of them have body parts that move. You will see automobiles, office and factory equipment, and how everything evolved over time. Some of the machinery will be in motion to show how they functioned. You will also see smaller items like fossils, precious stones, jewelry, and clothes. There is so much to see that no one can see it all in one visit," the man said as he smiled and patted Donovan on the back.

"What about the Door?" Donovan asked.

This time the man stared and with a grin, nodded. "Well, son, that's an amazing attraction too. Many people are drawn to it or come here just to see it. I'm sure you heard some things about it. That's on the eighth floor. Don't worry, you won't miss it. No, you certainly won't miss it." The man's gaze made Donovan a little nervous. He didn't know why, but he felt strange after that.

As the man was talking, the two groups were ushered into a large room on the right. Each group was assigned a guide. The guides reviewed the maps and emphasized some areas they thought they would really be interested in. But that decision is always up to the visiting parties. The guides first needed to know how long they planned on staying. The House Mothers indicated that their entire visit would be about seven hours. This included one hour for lunch and another hour for gift shopping. So that would leave about five hours for viewing. "That's great," one of the guides said. "Now let's see what's the best attractions to focus on with that amount of time."

After picking out the main things everyone agreed on, and since there were so many more things that they wanted to see but couldn't, the guides suggested that they could return within a month to see the rest. They said that if they returned within that time-frame, admission would be free. And they would receive another voucher for a free meal. If they returned after that, then admission would be half-price. The museum was especially compensating to children, the elderly, and the physically challenged.

All in all, there were eight floors. Even though there were artifacts on the first floor, it was the area where everyone gathered to get ready for the tour. There are plenty of restrooms, water fountains, and relaxation areas if anyone needs them. And the employee's stations are in the back.

The second, third, fourth, sixth, seventh, and eighth floors are for viewing. The fifth floor is where all the restaurants are, and huge rest areas, souvenir shops, and many restrooms. Even though the fifth floor is for shopping, each floor offers souvenirs. But the souvenirs on each floor are limited to that floor's displays only. There are also water fountains and rest areas on each floor but no places to buy meals. Eating is asked to be kept at a minimum on the major viewing floors. The museum tries to keep the artifacts as clean as possible since many of them can be touched.

The House Mothers decided that the first group would view floors six through eight and the second group would view floors two through four. Then everyone would meet on the fifth floor to have lunch. Donovan was ecstatic because the Door was located on the eighth floor, and he was in the second group. This way, he would see it in the last part of the tour. Hopefully, by that time, everyone would be so caught up or tired that they wouldn't notice if he slipped away. The only problem was how to get back to the bus on time. He will be at the top of the museum. So he decided that he would not ask any questions, and slip away early. Hopefully this would give him enough time to rejoin the group. Then Donovan heard something that gave him a jolt. It was the sound of a train. Suddenly, his dream came back to his remembrance.

A "whoop-woo" sound filled the air. "Awe, the train is here," one of the guides said.

No one seemed to notice the soft train tracks grooved into the floor. But sure enough, a huge caboose pushing two large boxed cars slowly crept upon them. "This is a little treat we offer our group tourists, especially when there are a lot of children. You will ride it through the first floor sites and then it will drop each group off at their destinations. But before we board, are there any final questions?", said the guide.

Donovan raised his hand.

"Yes, sir, how can we further assist you?" he asked.

Still a little shaken from the arrival of the train, Donovan quivered his words. "Well, I have heard that the museum has records of births. I mean of ordinary people, like me. And I heard that there are records of traumatic incidents that cause people to be left at orphanages. I was wondering if that was true. Cuz you didn't mention anything about that, and I really would like to know. See, some kids know how they came to live at the orphanage. But I don't, and no one seems to know or remember. Can I find that out here?"

The guide stared intensely as Donovan explained his situation. Donovan noticed the gaze and felt as though he should not have asked. He also noticed everyone was staring at him as well. He now felt that there was something someone didn't want him to know. And that it was something that no one was allowed to discuss. But why? He just couldn't understand.

The guide, noticeably nervous, stuttered and said, "Oh, yes, there is a room to research all of that. I'm sorry for the pause but no one usually asks about that on their first visit. They are usually more interested in the sights. All of that information is located here on the first floor. But I'm sure you don't want to spend your time going through that old stuff. You won't have time to see any of the sights if you do. Maybe someone can bring you back again if you all can't return in a month. Then you can take your time and look up whatever it is you are looking for." He patted Donovan on the back as he finished his response. Donovan smiled and nodded as he glanced around at everyone else. Just like his dream, they seemed frozen as they stood there, not moving or saying a word. Donovan didn't let on, but he now felt that he had to be careful. So he kept on smiling, and said, "Okay, I understand. Yes, maybe another time."

"Any more questions?" the guide bellowed. No one said anything. They just shook their heads. "Well if that is it, let's ride."

"All aboard," the conductor shouted.

"Come on," the guides waved. "The train will take everyone to their first destination." Again, Donovan thought about his dream. He began to shake and quiver. "Oh, no, now what is really about to happen?"

∼

One by one, everyone got on the train, one group in the front and one in the back. Donovan's group was to get off on the second floor because they were the first stop, so they all sat near the front of the train. Donovan sat in the first car but not by choice. It was left vacant. It was the same place where he sat in his dream.

But in his dream, the train wasn't as nice. This one had a fold-down tray in the front of the seat. The guides instructed them to pull the tray out because they were going to serve a snack before they took off. "Here's another complimentary gift. We like to make sure you don't get too hungry before lunch," one said. They passed out a paper bag that contained a small sandwich, veggie fries, and a fruit cup, and gave everyone their choice of water, milk or juice.

After everyone finished, one of the guides said, "Anyone need to use the restroom before we get started?" A few children got off with one of the Mothers and one of the guides assisting them. "Do you have to go to the restroom, young man," the other guide asked Donovan.

"No, sir," he replied. "Well, you seem like a responsible young man. Help me collect the trash and I will show you where to throw it away."

"Okay," Donovan replied.

When Donovan returned to his seat, the guide reached out to shake his hand. As Donovan shook his hand, they both received a tingle. "Oh, you shocked me," said the guide.

"I'm sorry. I do that from time to time." Donovan, puzzled as he spoke, noticed that the guide quickly drew back his hand and his right eye twinkled. "That's strange," he thought. The shock didn't seem that strong to him. "I didn't hurt you, did I?" Donovan asked.

"No, no, certainty not, son. It just took me by surprise." He backed up slowly and continued, "As long as you are okay, I'm okay."

"Yes, I'm good. I'm used to it," Donovan replied.

"Well, we are good, then. Yes, we are very good," the guide replied.

By this time, everyone was back on the train. The guide went to the back of the train and sat down with the other guide. Donovan turned around so he could continue to watch him. He saw him whisper to the other one. The other guide squinted his eyes and shook his head. But the one that whispered nodded his head. Then they both looked at Donovan, puzzled. Donovan turned away quickly, and mumbled, "What was that all about. It was just a shock. I didn't mean to do it. I can't help it. It just happens from time to time." He slid down in his chair hoping everything was truly okay.

"Alrighty then, everyone buckle up. We are about to take off. And in front of you, there is a small pocket with a pair of headphones. Take those out and plug them into the base of your seat. We will first circle the first floor. As we do that, the guides will tell you a few things about the exhibits," the conductor said.

Donovan closed his eyes and said, "I knew it, I just knew it. Oh boy, I'm really not sure I want to go on this tour, but it's too late to back out." He said a small prayer, "I don't know if anyone is listening and I'm not sure if anyone even cares. But if someone is listening, bless me and keep me safe. Then I will know for sure that someone is really there. And that someone does care." With that, he took a deep breath, opened his eyes and prepared to listen to the guides.

With two blasts of the train's whistle, it slowly began to move. Everyone marveled at the wonderful sights as the train moved along. Still wondering what was going on behind him, Donovan peeped around. Everyone eerily sat still as they glanced. He just turned back around and looked straight ahead as he continued to listen even though he couldn't really enjoy what the guides were saying. He was thinking about his dream. And what was going to happen once he got off the train? "Well, at least he wasn't getting off on the top level like in my dream," he thought. That gave him some comfort. And with that thought, he began to relax a little more.

Finally, the train reached the second floor. "First stop," the conductor yelled. "Okay, good people, this is where the first group gets off," he said.

So Donovan and his group, along with one House Mother and a guide, exited the train. "You all enjoy your visit," the conductor said. And with two blows of the whistle, the train moved on to drop off the other group.

∼

The area where the train let them off at is called the Depot. It is located in a hallway behind the main tourist section. There are benches, snack machines, and restrooms available; everything anyone needs to get themselves together before entering the exhibit area.

Across the hallway and a little to the right is a glass door with a sign above that says, ENTRANCE to the Main Exhibit. Together, everyone lined up and followed the guide through the door. The House Mother stayed at the rear to keep an eye on the children. When Donovan saw this, he wondered if she was going to stay behind the entire time. If so, that might pose a problem. But for now, it was too soon for him to be majorly concerned about it. The floor with the Door was a long way off. He just wanted to have fun because this day seemed as though it took forever to get here.

Once through those doors, it was like entering a whole new world. All Donovan could hear was the loud hustling and bustling of people and the activities going on. It was astonishing how he could hear none of this from the Depot. With a long expel of breath, Donovan said, "Wow, I wonder how they managed that?" He saw the look on everyone's face and could tell that they were wondering the same thing too.

There were people and artifacts everywhere. Not just tourist people but entertainers and vendors too. And their costumes were unimaginable. Each museum worker was dressed in a theme that represented something on that floor. People were doing some of everything like riding huge wheel bikes, fighting battles, and blowing glass. There was a small raceway with actually buggies racing. A little way down, there were different types of locomotives. There were replicas of animals as well as live ones. There were people in large glass tanks scuba diving for fossils and feeding fish. There was so much that it was hard to focus just on what the guide was talking about. Everyone's eyes, even the House Mothers, drifted away from the voice of the guide. And Donovan was glad that the House Mother was getting caught up in the excitement. This gave him more hope for slipping away.

∾

Soon, the time arrived for both groups to meet on the fifth floor. And it was just the right time, too. It was easy to see that everyone was growing tired and needed a break. For a first-time visit, it was very overwhelming. Plus, stomachs were starting to growl.

Both groups met and were excited to tell each other about their amazing experience. There was an area already sectioned off for them so that they could sit together. Everyone had the choice of what they wanted to eat. Most of the children chose fast food because they didn't get a lot of that where they lived. The orphanage made sure they ate as healthily as possible, but today was different. It was all about enjoying themselves while they learned.

"Souvenirs anyone? Anyone interested in a souvenir?"

To Donovan's surprise, it was a man walking around selling souvenirs related to the Door. Many vendors were walking around, but this man caught Donovan's attention because his items twinkled. They twinkled because they were made with bits of colored glassed encased in a glossy red wood-like door. And once he focused on the man, he could hear him say, "Get a piece of the Door and take it home with you."

Donovan's staring made the man take notice of him. He walked over and said hello to everyone and hello with a big smile to Donovan. "I see you staring, young man. Did something catch your eye?"

"Yes," Donovan replied. "Are those souvenirs really made from the Door?" he asked.

"No my son, they are just a reminder of the Door. No one can actually take a piece of it." As he talked, Donovan felt that the man had the most peaceable smile. And that made him feel very comfortable.

"Would you like one?" the man asked.

"Why, yes. I would like to have one that is hanging on a hook. This way I can wear it or hang it somewhere in my room," Donovan answered.

"Then that is exactly what you will have, my friend," the man replied. He reached into his bag and gave Donovan one that was wrapped in paper. He handed it to Donovan and as their hands touched, a tingly feeling occurred. Donovan stared into the man's eyes, and the man smiled. Neither of them said anything. But Donovan knew that they were still speaking. And it was a good feeling, but he didn't understand why. The last time he touched someone, it shocked them. He has shocked many people, but this time it was different. It was pleasant. He had never experienced that before. And with the look in the man's eyes, somehow, he knew that he would eventually find out.

"How much?" his House Mother asked.

"Oh, no cost, ma'am. This one is on me," the man replied.

"Well, isn't that sweet," the House Mother said to Donovan.

"It most certainly is," Donovan said. He shook the man's hand and emotionally said, "Thank you, sir."

"You are more than welcome," the man replied as he walked away.

Donovan turned around to everyone and held up his item, but he did not take it out of the paper. He just wanted them to see that he had it before he safely stuck it in his pocket. As he looked at the group, the two guides' eyes were wide open, almost fearful. That startled him. Again, he thought, "What is up with those two? They are strange." He looked away and decided that he would not interact with them unless it was absolutely necessary.

～

Once everyone picked out a keepsake, the two groups continued on. Donovan's heart began to flutter. This time, he would get to see the Door.

His group moved from floor to floor and finally they reached the last floor. The House Mother said, "Donovan, I know you are excited now that you will finally have a chance to see the Door."

It was hard for Donovan to act as though he wasn't interested. His face told all. It was flushed. Plus, that's all he had talked about at the orphanage. Then the guide said something that everyone thought was strange.

"House Mother, Donovan looks a little flushed. Do you think it is a good idea for him to continue to see the Door? I know he wants to, but the excitement may be too much for him. We don't want him to get sick." With a slight pause and a small sigh, he went on to say, "Well, I probably shouldn't tell you this, but I've heard stories about the Door and people who didn't feel well." Chuckling a little as he spoke, he said, "Of course, I haven't experienced it, but some of the other guides have. Never mind, as I said, I shouldn't tell you anymore."

The House Mother interrupted and said, "No, no, please go on."

Donovan stood there frozen as he listened to him. That's when he saw the guide slightly grin as the House Mother told him to continue. Donovan knew his grin was wicked, so he squinted his eyes and snarled a little. He never felt such anger toward anyone. He also knew that the guide was signaling him out and trying to prevent him from seeing the Door. But Donovan wasn't having it. A determination flared in him that made him want to fight for himself. He wasn't going to let anyone stop him from getting to see the Door. The first time he couldn't go to the museum because he was sick. Now, this guide was trying to prevent him.

As the guide continued to talk, he said that one of the children got so excited when he saw the Door, he collapsed. The child had to be carried out on a stretcher. So the museum asked the guides to signal out anyone whom they felt wasn't up to seeing the exhibit and to not let them go into the room where it was located.

The House Mother, very concerned, stared at Donovan and said, "Don, do you think you should sit out this part? I know you have been waiting to see it, but if it is too much for you to handle, it is okay. Just let me know." Donovan, with a firm but not too serious look, politely said, "No House Mother." Honestly, I'm fine." Then he smiled.

"Are you sure, Don? I don't want the museum to get in trouble. And I don't want the orphanage to be upset with me. But, most importantly, I don't want anything to happen to you. You are irreplaceable."

"No, I'm fine. I assure you," he replied. "Please, House Mother, have I ever lied to you? Trust me, please, just trust me."

"Okay, but if you feel weak, let me know," she said.

"I will. I promise," Donovan said with another smile as he softly hugged her. And as he hugged her, he looked at the guide and squinted again to let him know that he was on to him. And whatever he was up to, it didn't work. As the guide looked back at Donovan, he too squinted. At this point, they both knew where each other stood.

For the rest of the tour, Donovan did not walk close to the guide. He could feel Donovan's tension and would peep his way every now and then. Donovan wouldn't smile at him and could now see some fear in the guide's eyes. The guide knew that Donovan was growing stronger. The closer they got to the Door, the more nervous the guide seemed. As for Donovan, he was thinking about his dream. He now believed that his dream was not just a dream but a warning. Someone wanted to scare him so he would run away. But unlike in his dream, he decided not to run. He believed that if he did not face whatever it was, he would be running and hiding for the rest of his life. He would never find out why he was being chased or why the guide seemed to be picking on him. Plus, he would never know the true story about the Door.

Oddly, the closer they came to where the Door was located, the fewer the number of people they saw. Some were leaving from that area, but not many were visiting. The Door is located in a room at the far end of a narrow hallway that branched off of the main floor. And it was kept in a room all by itself. "That is interesting," Donovan thought. "Why is the Door so far away from everything else? And why is it the only thing in the room? Maybe it is humongous," he chuckled. Donovan's excitement began to make him feel giddy. He couldn't stop smiling. The more he thought, the wider his smile became.

"Maybe people are afraid to go down there since there have been so many strange stories surrounding it. Because even though the hallway is well lit, it still looked spooky. Or maybe they were just not as interested in seeing it. The museum is huge and by the time they got to the Door, they might have been too tired to walk any farther. So they felt as though they could skip that part." These types of thoughts ran through Donovan's head.

He noticed that there were people looking down that way. Some even pointed but shook their heads and walked on. "Well, maybe the anticipation was too much for some to handle like the guide said, so they didn't want to get sick." Whatever the reason, Donovan didn't care. This was the moment he had been waiting for.

He also realized that he was not going to be able to sneak away, so he decided to be bold and ask all of his questions while he was there. If he couldn't get the answers he wanted, it wouldn't be because he hadn't tried.

~

Together, they went down the narrow hallway and stopped outside the room where the Door was kept.

"Well, this is it everyone. The moment some of you have been eagerly waiting for," the guide said. They all smiled and chuckled as they glanced at Donovan. "Now this is as far as I'm going to go. I will not go inside with you because I've been here so much that I don't desire to hear the speech again. However, there is a gentleman inside who will give you some history about the Door. I will be outside when you are ready to leave." Donovan was glad to hear that. He felt as though no one would stop him from finding out what he wanted to know.

As they entered the room, it felt like a gentle breeze was stirring. And everyone began to murmur that they could hear soft noises. "Maybe the breeze is coming from the windows," someone said. But as they looked around, there weren't any open windows. And all the windows were high up.

"Maybe it's coming from the vents. Maybe it was all over the museum the entire time, but no one paid it any attention due to everything else going on. The commotion had simply drowned the noise out," another one said.

But still the sounds seemed strange. As they listened, the noise sounded more like whispering. It was beginning to make everyone feel uncomfortable. And it didn't help when Donovan said out loud, "It sounds like people are whispering in here. But I don't see anybody."

Suddenly, a lanky man, with a somewhat large pointy nose that held up his glasses, came from a door in the back. "Well, hello, everyone," he said. "Come on in. I'm Mr. Peeker. That's P-E-E-K-E-R." They all chuckled. "Why, yes, it is kind of a funny name. It sounds like I'm always watching something or somebody. And in a sense, that it true. I watch the Door. But a person who peeps, that's P-E-E-P-S, doesn't want others to know that he or she is looking. I'm just the opposite. I want everyone to know that I am keeping a close watch on the Door. So, while my name may sound like I'm sneaky, I really am not. Now, come on in and make yourselves at home. You have just entered to wonderful world of the Door."

∾

Donovan, with him imagination running rapid, wondered why he must watch the Door. It wasn't like anyone could steal it without being noticed. It's way too big. The Door stood about twenty feet tall. Its frame has leafy vine patterns carved in it. It is a double door and about fourteen feet wide. It is deep red in color yet somewhat translucent. It has iridescent spots on it that seems to twinkle. And no two spots seem the same. From the spots runs bluish-red streaks like veins connecting each spot to the other. It is a beautiful yet odd sight to see.

The Door sits on a roped-off platform. And as they moved closer to it, the sounds seem a tad bit louder. But over top of it is a huge fan hanging from a vent. This could be where the noise is coming from.

The House Mother said hello and told the man where they were from.

"Oh, that is wonderful," the man replied. "I too grew up in a village and lived there for many years. One day, I also visited the museum. It was not as fancy then, but still, it was very interesting and the main attraction to those visiting the town. The town wasn't as large either because life was simpler then. But things have changed. Yep, things are ever-evolving. And as the villages grew, so did the town and, therefore, did the museum.

"I'm sure you have already heard that the museum keeps a record of the town's events. Actually, the town was developed because of the villages. The need for things changed and the need grew in great demand. So the town people figured out how to do things that weren't being done by the villagers, like recordkeeping. Other lands were getting assistance in their time of need because they could give an account of their loss during devastating occurrences. The recordkeepers realized that to receive funding, they needed to record not only everyone's names but also when they were born, where they live, what they did for a living and so forth and so forth. This way everyone could be validated.

"For example, let's look at the cattle ranchers. The recordkeepers needed to know how much it cost to maintain the ranch, how much milk and meat is produced, and so forth. This required the ranchers to keep a record of what they were doing so they could provide the needed information. From this need came the need to have people go from house-to-house collecting information. Then came the need to have a place where all this information would be kept. This is how our Data Hall building became established. The hall is also the place where everyone comes together to discuss things as the need changes and the place where all the information is kept surrounding the changes.

"Now, hopefully, you can see why this type of function did not need to be done in the village: because the villages are basically made up of farms and factories. And each village does not need its own Data Hall since they are an extension of one another. There just needs to be one place where everyone can go to see how everything connects as one. So this is how the town came into existence. And, as a need occurred, a building was established. Even though people live in the town and have businesses here, the villages are still highly regarded. They are the life-source from which everything began. Plus, the villages are the main source of food and goods. The town is the focal point for bringing those goods, since most of the restaurants, cafeterias, etc. rely on their supplies.

"Many people from the villages come to the town excited because it is quite different. But what I always tell them is that without the resources from the villages, we would struggle. The villages provide our main source of things like coal, wool, tobacco, cotton, and, of course, foods like meats, fruits, and vegetables. Our factories turn their resources into products. So we need each other. Therefore, do not feel less than if you live in the village all your life. We need people to stay there to produce for the rest of us.

"The villages are also our main source of wood. As a matter of fact, there is a certain part of land where the trees grow, the wood is like none other. The bark is extremely hard; so, when a tree is cut down, it must be sliced in the woods. The trunk is way too heavy to transport whole. No one has developed equipment strong enough to pick up the entire tree. It is almost totally fire and weather resistant. It is not indestructible, but it can take a lot of friction before it is worn down. And that, my dear guests, brings us to the Door.

"We believe that the Door was originally made from one of those trees. When we got the door, it was a part of a burning home. The home belonged to a wealthy banker who swindled a lot of people. Some says that the banker set it on fire and some believe that others set it on fire. But what everyone does know is that he was arrested and let out on bail. He had assured the court that he could return most of the money in exchange for a lighter punishment. He said that the money was hidden and that he would return within a few short hours. But, when he didn't, a bail bondman was sent to retrieve him. When the bondman's arrived at the home, he discovered the house on fire. By the time the firefighters arrived, the home was almost totally destroyed. Amazingly, the Door was perfectly intact. It was sweaty from the heat but not scorched at all. It was a little silty, but as the hose put the fire out, the Door washed clean. It began to shine bright and twinkle almost as it was smiling, happy that it was out of danger.

"'Wow,' one of the firefighters said. 'Look at it! It is still intact. And I remember this home from when I was younger. My dad and I had to go to a camp leader's home for a sleepover. The Door made an impression on me and my dad. The leader said that he moved here after a councilman abandoned his home. He had stolen funds from the governing body and fled to keep from being prosecuted. They auctioned off everything, and I was looking to buy a house. When I saw the Door, it impressed me so much that I had to have it. And everyone who comes here admires it. Now that was such a long time ago,' the firefighter said."

"After examining the Door, the people felt that it would be a nice addition to the museum. And that's how the Door ended up here. Any questions?"

Of course, Donovan eagerly raised his hand.

"Yes, sir," the man replied.

"Well, I have heard that there were mysteries surrounding the Door. What is that all about? And why is the Door in a room by itself? And why are people fainting? And why aren't there more people coming down to see it? And why...?"

"Wait a minute, wait a minute," the man replied, giggling. "One question at a time. I can see where you are going with your questions, and I think that I can answer them all. But, first, I must say that it is so lovely to have someone who is interested in the Door. It's been a long time since anyone has been so excited. I, too, was a lad when I visited the museum and had several questions. There were rumors then, and I too was curious. Now let me share with you what I have found out and if you have any more questions, I will do my best to help you."

~

The man continued, "When the Door was initially brought to the museum, it was placed in the center of the floor. Because of the rumors, the museum hoped it would bring in more tourists. One rumor was that it was thought to have been around since the beginning of time. Well not the Door, but the wood. First of all, the wood is somewhat translucent. You can even see some of the rings. That in itself is odd. It is estimated to have over one hundred rings. Keep in mind that every ring represents about ten years. So, when the Door was made, the wood had to be at least one thousand years old. And there has not been another tree exactly like it. This rumor, along with stories of the people who lived in the house with the Door, made it quite mysterious.

"At that time, the museum only had five floors. It was placed on the fifth floor so that the people would hopefully visit each floor before getting to it. The strange thing is that as people would walk past the Door, and small accidents would occur. It happened so much that the Door developed a bad reputation for being jinxed, so it was moved to the back end of the floor. Then when the workers came in the next day, it seemed as though the other items were pushed forward, like the Door didn't want anything near it. Each time they moved or rearranged something, the same thing would happen. That's when one of the museum workers remember a story about a mover who helped to transport the Door to the museum.

"Every time the mover touched the Door, he would be mildly shocked. At first, he thought it was a coincidence. But when he went to lean on the Door, to help secure the support straps, a surge shocked him so strong that it thrusted him back a few feet. When he was helped up, he tried to speak but could only stutter. They took him to the hospital. As he was being carried away, he kept blinking his eyes and mumbling as if he was trying to tell them something. When he recovered, his coworkers asked him what was trying to say, but he couldn't remember.

"One of then reminded him of how he was bad mouthing the Door. He said that he shouldn't have told the Door it was a door from hell. That is why it could take so much heat and survive. He said that the Door didn't like what he said, and it didn't want him to touch it. They all laughed, but the injured mover said, 'Naw, man. That ain't it at all. I shock things all the time that no one else does. This Door must contain a lot of substance, which my body can't take. Who really knows what makes wood, anyway? And no one knows what was put on that Door to maintain it. I am just more susceptible to things than others. I've always known that my body was different. I guess I just have more electrical juice than the normal person. Plus, I don't believe in that kind of stuff.'

'Well, you are sure right about having more of some things than other people because you have a filthy mouth,' another responded. 'And if our buddy is right, you met your match with the Door.'

'Naw, man, like I said, I don't believe in that. There's a logical answer that can explain everything. We just don't know what the answers are. But as for my mouth, you better know it! I will get you straight! I've had to straighten my wife out a few times. But not just with my mouth, with my fist also.' He chuckled.

'Okay, keep that mess up if you want to,' the first man said. 'I don't care what anyone says, things have a way of coming back on you. And when it does, it doesn't always come back the way you put it out. It happens when you never expect it and it comes back worse. That jolt almost killed you. Look at you! Your hair has turned white and your face is wrinkled. You may have hit your wife a few times, but she still looks good. You look a mess.'

'Aw, man, go ahead with that stuff,' he responded. They dropped the subject in the room but everyone else was talking about what had happened. And the mover may have said that he didn't believe in weird things like that; but, I heard that he even started being nicer to his wife.

"After the museum worker told the story, they thought that the Door could possibly have an extraordinary amount of energy radiating from it. That's how the Door ended up in a room by itself. But even with moving the Door to its own room, strange things still happened."

"What kind of strange things?" someone asked.

"Oh, several things. Let me see what I can tell before it is time for you all to leave."

~

The story continued. "Well, there was a ticket-taker working here. It was discovered that she was taking artifacts and selling them. The museum knew things were missing, but they could never seem to catch the person. One reason they had a hard time catching her was because she was one of the people on the team who was supposed to be on the lookout for the culprit. So, no one was watching her."

"I thought the museum had cameras," Donovan said.

"Why, yes, it does. That was another concern. The cameras did not pick up anything. Well, come to find out, the ticket-taker had moved here from another region. She changed her identity because she was wanted for stealing there as well. She worked for a security company, and they could not find out how someone was going into people's homes, taking things and not being filmed. Later, it was determined that she knew how to manipulate the cameras. When the museum found this out, they began to watch her secretly.

"Once they had proof, the head of the museum, along with the police, came out to arrest her. They didn't want to make the arrest while the visitors were present, so they waited until all the visitors left.

"Now another worker overheard the head as he was devising his plan. She didn't hear who he was talking about, but she'd heard enough. As she was changing her clothes to go home, she told another worker of what she heard. Unfortunately, the person she told was the one to be arrested. She told the ticket-taker that she didn't know who it was, but that it was going to happen that night.

"As the ticket-taker listened, she devised a plan to get away. With her security knowledge, she would trick the cameras one more time. She would pause them long enough to hide out and make everyone think she left before the arrest could be made. She decided to hide in the room with the Door.

"The other worker told her to come on because she wanted to see who it was being arrested. The ticket-taker told her to go ahead and she would meet up with her in a minute. When she thought the worker was out of sight, she went to fix the cameras, then quietly crept up the hallway to hide. But what she didn't know was that the worker returned to get something she'd forgotten. As the worker returned to the locker room, she saw the ticket-taker coming out of the surveillance room. She started to yell but thought it was strange. So she followed her instead. She saw her go into the room with the Door. She went to the door to peep in but did not go in all the way. She was always afraid of the Door because of the rumors. As she looked in, she saw smoke. "Why was it smoky in there?" she thought. She gave a quick yell to her, but no one answered. She ran in fear that something was wrong. As she exited the building, the head of the museum and the police entered. The head asked her if she had seen the ticket-taker. Startled by his question, she now knew that the ticket-taker was the thief. That explained the strange behavior. Trying to catch her breath, she told the head that she last saw her go in the room where the Door was located. She went home tearful because the ticket-taker was her friend. She felt sorry for her and believed that she must have had a good reason for stealing. If she had known she needed help, maybe the two of them could have lived together. By telling on her, she felt as though she had betrayed her friend.

"The next day when she went to work, she found that her friend was not caught. Again, the head approached her with more questions. They believed that the young lady had helped the ticket-taker get away by saying she was in the room where the Door was located. Over and over, she insisted she had nothing to do with it. She explained how she had forgotten something and when she returned, she saw the ticket-taker coming out of the surveillance room. She thought it was strange, so she followed her. And that was all. She said the reason why she was so out of breath when they saw her was because she saw smoke in the room. She was just trying to get out safely. The head, looking puzzled said, 'Smoke? What smoke? There was no smoke when we checked.' Tearfully, the young girl insisted that she was innocent. She said, 'It's that Door. It's something strange about that Door. It must be. People are always disappearing. It's not me, it's that Door!'

⁓

"Wow, that is scary," several in the group said.

"Let me tell you one more, then I'll tell you one about me. My story is not scary.

"This next story is about two sisters. But before I go on, are there any questions?"

"No, no, please go on," everyone insisted. "This is better than going to the movies," another said. "Alrighty then, but this one is pretty gruesome. So stop me if it is too much for you.

⁓

"There were two sisters who lived on the outskirts of a village and had been raised very harshly by their grandmother. Their mother had left them with her a long time ago. They didn't remember their mother. They only remember what their grandmother had said about her.

'She came from my womb, but she did not come from my heart. She was a bad girl, a very naughty girl. She did so many unmentionable things. One day, she ran away. I thought I had seen the last of her but then a knock came to the door. When I opened the door, there you two were and no one else in sight, a product of my daughter's filth. I don't even know if you have the same father. But you two are not going to be like her. Oh, no, and I'm going to make sure of that.'

"They had heard that story over and over again especially when they were being punished. They were constantly reminded that their mother was no good. And the grandmother's way of preventing that action in them was to flog them and not let them out of her sight. They missed so many days out of school that eventually they stopped going. When the grandmother was asked why they were not attending, she replied, 'Homeschooling is the best schooling.' After a while people stopped asking. No one saw the girls, and no one questioned why.

"Some years later, people began to see the two girls. When asked how they were doing, they would reply, 'Very well, thank you.'

'And your grandmother?'

'Oh, she is old now, and we are taking care of her.'

"Then neighbors would notice how well kept their grounds began to appear, nothing like before. Before it was trashy with a lot of overgrown brush. But now, each time someone would pass by, they could tell that it was being cleaned up. One saw a young man working on the grounds, hauling things away. When the sisters were seen again, the neighbor asked if either of them had gotten married. They both replied no. The neighbor then said that she had not meant to pry, but she had noticed a young man on the premises.

'Well, yes. he is our Hand,' the sisters said in unison. 'We have been wanting to do things differently.'

'Oh, well, how do you pay for all that labor? He's painting and mending and all sorts of things. Does he work in exchange for room and board?' she asked.

"With the sisters slightly glancing at each other, one said, 'Oh, I thought you didn't want to pry. But if you must know, yes, he does. We have a little money coming in as well. We take care of a few of our elderly relatives. They came to stay and decided not to leave. Getting old, you see, they thought it would be best if they lived all in one place. So we get paid to take care of them. That way we use the excess money to fix up the house.'

'Oh, that is wonderful,' the neighbor said. 'And truly I meant no harm in asking. It's just that we haven't seen either of you in such a long time. And now that you are coming around, people were hoping that we all could be back in relationship with each other. I'm sorry if I offended you.'

"Softly smiling, they said, 'Yes, maybe so. But not grandma and the others. They are housebound, so they can't come around.'

'Oh, that's understandable,' she replied. 'Well, don't be strangers. We want to see you at some of the functions. As a matter of fact, there is one coming up in a few weeks at my house. I do hope that you can attend. And since neither of you are married, there might be a few young men interested in seeing you as well,' she giggled.

"Again, the two glancing at each other said, 'We will see.'

'Well, I do hope so. I will send you more information in a few days,' she said as she walked off smiling and waving.

"After a few days passed, the neighbor decided to drop off the invitations instead of mailing them. She thought that she could visit with the grandmother while she was there. When she arrived, she knocked but no one answered. So when she saw the hand, she asked about the sisters. He said that they had gone to run some errands and to see the banker but would be back later today or tomorrow. He hoped that they would have returned today.

When the neighbor asked about the grandmother, he had no idea of what she was talking about. He hadn't seen anyone other than the sisters since he started working here. He said, 'I've been all over that house except for the basement. And I'm pretty sure, no one's in there. Anyway, that's their private workspace. They make something down there, and they are very secretive about it. They said that I should never go there if I want to stay here. They don't want anything disturbed or it may cost them to lose money. So I said I wouldn't go down there, and I don't. I don't know what they are doing, but it must be very lucrative. They always have plenty of money. And that's all that matters to me. I have a roof over my head and money in my pockets. I like it here. It's quiet. See, I've drifted for a long time and I wanted to find somewhere I could put down my roots. I mind my own business and do what they say. They don't mess with me and I don't mess with them.'

"Startled by what he was saying, she began to briskly walk away, nervously shaking and knees buckling.

'What's the matter with you lady?' he yelled.

"But she didn't answer him. She composed herself enough to get in her car and left.

"After she got home, she began to tell her husband about what had taken place, from meeting the girls up until meeting the hand. The husband assured her that she was making more out of things than what it was. He agreed for them to visit the banker early the next day. He too needed to talk with him about not receiving his dividend check.

"When he and his wife visited the banker, the house was on fire. They were looking around for the banker, but he was nowhere to be found. Even more surprisingly, they had one of the sisters in the ambulance.

"Why was she there? Where was the other sister? Had the banker did something to her? Had the sister come to look for her? Why was the house on fire? What in the world was going on, they thought. They spoke with a policeman to try to find out what happened.

"He explained that there was warrant for the banker. The bail bondman came to retrieve him and found the house ablaze but did not see the banker. The young lady was holding onto the bottom of a tree. It was strange because it seemed as though she had been there for quite some time. She was wet. And it rained the night before. We figured she's been there all night, but we don't know why. She's not talking, sort of in a state of shock. Just staring at the house. We had to pry her from around the tree, and she began to scream and point. So we sedated her. Maybe we will find out what happened after we get her to calm down. She must have seen something, and it frightened her so much that she ran and hid, afraid to go any farther. 'Why are you people here?' the policeman asked.

"'Well, we are here looking for the banker...' They told the policeman everything that they knew. To make the story a little shorter, the police investigated the sisters' home. All seemed normal until they went into the basement. There they found the grandmother's corpse. It was bad enough that the woman had been murdered and not buried, but the body had been chopped and woven back together. She must have seen her death coming because her face showed that she died in fear. There is a deep gash in her back where she had been stuffed and resewn.

"Then there was another woman's corpse, which had been mutilated and restored. It was later determined that this was their biological mother. There were two male corpses as well which were mutilated but not restored. They were kept in plastic. The men may have been their fathers. No one knows for certain, but it was felt that the sisters retaliated on everyone who had hurt them. We believe that they hated their grandmother, mother, and their fathers. We don't know this for certain, but we do know that at one time they were all living together because their social security checks were coming there. This is the money the girls were living on. The people had been dead for a while, but the checks were still coming.

"The sister holding on to the tree went to the prison mental institution. She still doesn't talk much, and her speech is very garbled. But one thing she says clearly, and she says it quite often."

"What is that?" they wanted to know.

"The Door. She repeatedly says, the Door."

"Wow, that was scary," they said.

"Now, I will tell you my story."

~

The group listened as he began to speak. "I was twelve when I first came to the museum. I had been coming into town selling goods with my father long before that. As a young fellow, I had always heard things about the Door. I was so spooked that I told my father that I never wanted to see it. My dad smiled, looked at me, and said, 'You will never have to worry about that.'

'Why?' I asked.

'Do you remember how your sister was about to fall into the creek? You asked her to grab your hand so you could pull her up. Remember, she wanted you to get me because she didn't feel that you were strong enough? And you told her it would take too long. So she grabbed your hand and you pulled her to safety.'

'Of course, I do,' I told him.

'And remember how you were able to get the young calf out of the thicket bush?'

Again, I said I remembered.

'Well, that mother cow was raging some kind of bad, but you still went to help. You risked getting hurt by the heifer. But, somehow, she stayed calm as you got her calf free. Son, you have a way with things. If there is any truth to the stories, I don't think it will bother you.'

"Well. when I was eleven, my father had an accident and could not go to the town. I assured the family that I was able to do what my father did by myself. On the day that I went, I had just turned twelve years old. My mother said that I was an adult now, and this is my first adult responsibility. I spoke with my dad to see what advise he had. Before I left the room, he grabbed my arm and said, 'Son, before you come home, why don't you visit the museum.' Even though he was smiling, he had a strange look on his face. I told him that I wasn't interested in going, but he reminded me that I was always having a dream where I would see myself in a suit and tie. He said that I was a great farmhand, but there are six more children here. Maybe the dream is telling you that your destiny is not on the farm but in the town. The museum has so many things; you might see something that you would like to do other than this. Plus, the museum has a way of answering many questions. You have always had so many questions. You just might find the answers there.

I assured my dad that I would never leave him nor Mom. He patted my hand and said, 'Son, just do what I ask.' So I made a promise that I would.

"As I was leaving home, everyone was standing around to see me off with my father waving from a window. It felt strange, as if they weren't expecting me to come back. That made me more nervous than going to town by myself.

"While in town, I had a great sale. I mean, extremely good. I was so excited to get back home to let my family know how well I did. After I got everything packed up, I remembered the promise I made to my father. It was getting late, and the museum was about to close. I initially thought that I would just tell my dad that the museum was closed, but I didn't like lying, so I went in.

"Most people were leaving when I purchased my ticket. As I went in, the doorkeeper asked, 'Are you sure you want to come in? The museum is about to close.' It seemed as though he didn't want to let me in, but I told him I wouldn't be long. Plus, I had just bought my ticket and the sign said, 'No refunds, can only exchange for another day.' As I squeezed past him, he yelled, 'Well, you didn't have to push me so hard.' I didn't think that I had. I was thinking to myself that he wouldn't move, and I was in a hurry. But, when I looked back, he was on the floor. I heard him tell the ticket seller that I knocked him down. But I knew I hadn't. He was overly exaggerating. He was someone like my father had told me about. Some people need a lot of attention especially when they don't have their way. They need to make a scene to look as if they'd been wronged. But, in reality, they can't admit that they are wrong.

"With so little time, I focused on the farming section. I wanted to see how far we had advanced. But a thought came to me to find out what I could about the Door. So I hurried up to the floor. It was almost empty. The woman at the door told me to come on in. She talked to me for a while and just like all of you, I had many questions. She, too, said that she believed that the rumors were true, but they weren't true for her. She said that when she came, the man told her to touch the Door. It would have a warm vibrating feel to it. So she did, and it did. After she touched it, she decided that she wanted to work at the museum to help others with their fears.

"Then, she asked me to touch it. I was nervous, but I did. And just like she said, the Door had a warming feel to it, very soothing. At that moment, I felt that the Door had been misunderstood. Instead of fearing it, I wanted to safeguard it. I was so excited that I overcame my fear, and I couldn't wait to tell my father.

"When I returned home, it was late. Most everyone was in bed except for my mom and dad. And the strange thing about that was that my dad was moving around quite well. I said, 'Hey, I see you are much better.'

"'Yes,' he said.

"I told them how well I did with the goods and gave them the money. They were extremely pleased. I started to go to bed, but my dad asked me if there was anything else that I had to say. It was like he knew what I was feeling inside. Playfully, I said, 'What do you mean?'

"'You know,' he responded. 'Did you visit the museum?'

"'Yes,' I replied. 'I was going to tell you about that tomorrow.'

"'Well, if you are not too tired, your mother and I have waited this long for your safe return, we can wait a little longer.'

"So I told him that he was right and that I think that I would like to work at the museum. When I said that, they both looked at each other and smiled. My dad said that it was my decision. So when I turned twenty-one, I came to town to see if there was a position at the museum. I worked many assignments until the lady who kept the Door retired. That's how I started working here. And I have never been happier. I go back to the farm on holidays. Since I left, I have married and have a few children of my own. But I love what I do here. And I am glad that my father encouraged me to take that step.

"Now, do I believe the stories about the door? Yes, I do. Call it strong energy, negative energy, or bad energy. Call it whatever you want. But I do caution people about the Door. The Door has a way of dealing with people."

Donovan raised his hand and asked, "Well, how do you know if you have negative energy?"

"Energy comes from within the heart. If the heart is good, you will give off good energy. But if the heart is evil, you will give off bad energy. Are you basically good or bad, is the question? That's where you have to be truthful with yourself because somehow the Door knows," he said.

Donovan said that he knew that he wasn't perfect but believed he was good.

"No one is perfect son. But are you more good than bad?" he asked.

"Goooood," Donovan slurred.

"Well, that's all that matters. I tell you what, come touch the Door, and see what you feel. If you get a small shock, you may need to do better. But if you don't, you are on the right track," he said.

Slowly, Donovan approached the Door and cautiously touched it. While stretching toward it, he nervously closed his eyes. In the background, he could hear Mr. Peeker saying, "Don't be afraid, son. Just relax and everything will be okay." And as he got close to touching it, the noises he first heard seemed loud again. This time they were clearly whispering. When he touched the Door, a warm sensation occurred. This made Donovan smile. "Yes, it does feel warm," he said.

He could also feel the Door pulling him to the point where he couldn't remove his hand. Then, he went into a trance. He tried to mumble, but he couldn't. The noises became even louder. They weren't whispering anymore. They were conversing.

Suddenly, Donovan opened his eyes, but he did not see the Door any longer. He saw the appearance of people doing things. People that the stories were about. He saw the banker running and laughing, saying that he had enough money and that he could go away and no one would ever find him. He ran into his home to pack his things and the money. He entered the home so fast that the Door did not completely close behind him. Up to his porch came a young lady. She had heard him and realized that she and others had been betrayed. She confronted the banker. He told her that she had some nerve questioning his morals where she and her sister were guilty of their own crimes. He slapped her, and they began to scuffle. He could see another young lady running toward them from the outside. But before she could reach the porch, the two fell onto the frame of the Door. They froze and screeched. They turned translucent red with fire blazing from within them. Then, the Door absorbed them. After it did, it blew out a huge blaze of fire. The home combusted into flames. The young lady outside screamed in horror and ran into the yard, hiding behind a huge tree and crying hysterically as the bondsman arrived.

He could see the man who ridiculed the Door. He was a cruel, savage man. He was abusive to his wife and children. And many of his neighbors found him to be unbearable. He was a loudmouth on the job and kept a lot of trouble brewing. He saw where the Door did not like him and spewed him away. He could see the Door blowing dark smoke on him as a sign of its disapproval. Even though the man nor anyone else could see the smoke.

He saw the young ticket-taker and all the devilish things she had done over the years; all of the people she had stolen from and all the hurt it caused. He saw how she was amazed with the Door. After she entered the room, she touched it. It was so beautiful, and she wished that she could take it too. But that was her mistake. So the Door absorbed her as well.

He saw the Scout leader and the unmentionable things he did to the children, especially the boys. One day, he went as far as to kill a child to hide his crimes. After disposing of the body, he leaned on the Door post because he felt that he had covered all points of his atrocities. When he did, the Door screeched loud and consumed him.

He saw many people and the acts they did before the Door consumed them. But he also saw Mr. Peeker. He was smiling with his hands open. He called Donovan's name and said, "I've been waiting to meet you. Just like me, you were drawn to the Door for a reason. You are a good person and are chosen to watch the Door. Only good people like you can do this. When I came here, I, too, found that this was my mission after I touched the Door. I was chosen to take the place of the lady here before me. Just as you have been chosen to be my successor.

"The Door was originally a tree when a cursed man stumbled on it. His name was Tertsrick and he was a Trickster. He was initially put in place to oversee and help people. He had power that no one else had. But the Great Spirit, creator of all life, cursed him when he became evil. He was supposed to teach the chosen one how to take his place. But he didn't want that and thought that he could outsmart the Great Spirit. He wanted to live forever. So he killed the chosen one. This infuriated the Great Spirit, and it transformed him into a clear substance. He was told that he would live forever but in the form of the first thing he touched. Tertsrick stumbled on a tree stump. He and the tree became one.

"But Tertsrick didn't stumble over the stump by accident. The tree also grew against the will of the Great Spirit. The Great Spirit is the Creator of all things and has a will for everything. The tree knew that it was special. It was a part of a species of trees that were better built than other trees. So this tree wanted to be even better than all the trees of its kind.

"It moaned and moaned as it pushed itself outward, trying to be thicker than the rest. But instead of becoming larger in size, it actual caused a part to grow from its side. Before the piece grew too huge, the Great Spirit struck it and caused the outgrowth to fall off, leaving only a stump. The tree groaned even more because it was disfigured. It also knew that the Great Spirit was not finished with it. And It wasn't. It told the tree that it would become the most desirable but at a high cost for its disobedience.

"So the tree shook because it had no idea what was going to happened next. And it also was sorry for what it had done but it knew that it was too late to turn back. For once the Great Spirit curses something, it cannot be reversed.

"Therefore, the Great Spirit guided Tertsrick to the stump. Tertsrick did not even notice the tree trembling because the entire forest was in distress. All living things could tell something horrible was taking place. But the Great Spirit did not reveal its plan to anyone or anything.

"After the two became one, the tree groaned loud. It did not like Tertsrick being a part of it. And it now knew that it would be able to absorb anything that was disobedient. So both got what they wanted but not how they wanted it. Tertsrick would live forever, and the tree is the most desirable tree in the forest.

"The villagers could feel the tremble and hear the moaning. They had never heard anything like that before, so they fled to the coast in fear. Once the noise quieted, the people returned to the village. That's when the Great Spirit spoke to them for the first time. It was not displeased with them, but It made them leave the place. The place provided all means of living with the people having to do little to sustain life. They were no longer allow that luxury. Eventually, they settled and life went on. But never as easy as it was from the beginning.

"Now the tree was also angry that Tertsrick was a part of it. So its anger inside became a constant burning fire. This fire would torture Tertsrick continuously. No one could tell what was going on inside of the tree. They could only tell from the outside that the tree was odd and beautiful.

"Because the tree was so different, it was cut down and made into a door. The builder wanted it for his own home. He was rich and wanted the most extravagant home, and he believed this odd wood would make his house different than anyone else's. But the tree was extremely hard to cut. So he only created a door and its frame.

"As the builder had hoped, the Door was truly the talk of the villages. But even back then, it developed a reputation. If you had a foul mouth or something highly immoral about you, as you walked past the Door, it would give you a shock or a shove. This is the way it warned people to stay away because it didn't want to absorb anything else. It will also push away items that have been used for evil. That is why some of the items kept being moved at the museum.

"Since Tertsrick was inside, he wanted other people to be punished. So he would call out trying to get people's attention in hopes that they were evil and henceforth absorbed. See, there is a saying that says, misery loves company. And he was truly miserable. He couldn't reach out and grab people, but he could see them. But from the outside, the calling only sounds like strange noise to most people.

The iridescent spots on the Door are the eyes of the individuals. This is why no two spots look the same. There is even one spot that is reddish-black. That is Tertsrick's damaged eye.

"Since the tree regretted its actions, it wanted to do something good. It will allow anyone good to touch it. It wanted someone to watch it and help keep evil away. That is what it did for me one day. It showed me that you would come and take my place, and I can go home and be with my family. And when you have a family, you can share this secret with your most trusted loved ones. This secret was given to my father. That is why he encouraged me to come all those years earlier. I later realized that my father wasn't hurt. It was that I needed to make this journey for myself to find my destiny. That is why my name is Peeker. I am the keeper of the Door.

"Even though the Door is trying to do good, it needs help. The others inside are like Tertsrick. They are trying to lure people. So the Door needs someone who can watch it as much as possible and warn them if they are not good to Touch Not.

"As for you, my son, your name is Reesa, which means you are a Seer. The Door told me that a Seer would take my place and that I would know him when he could hear the voices talking. The voices of those who will forever be punished for their crimes. And they too can tell that you are good, extremely good. They know that you know their shame.

"Just like the guide who wouldn't come in. He is correct. He's been in here before and received a nice shock. So he won't come near the Door. He feels that the Door somehow knows something about him. That is why he was constantly focusing on you. You gave him the same feeling that the Door did, and he didn't like it. He will stay away from me, too. These types of people are devious and easily frightened. And rightfully so because they do so much wrong. They are always afraid something is going to get them.

"Now I know that you have a secret within yourself. You wonder how you got to the orphanage. This I can't tell you. You may be able to find it in our books or at the Hall. Some births were hidden for various reasons. And the orphanages allow people to drop off children without question. If you can't find out, then my suggestion is to not let that bother you. You are well-loved where you are. You have been chosen for a great responsibility. You will have a wonderful life and a chance to be a father yourself. So don't worry about the past. Just stay focused on the future, and you will not be disappointed.

"I also know that you had a dream. In your dream, you are always desiring to come to the museum, but something frightens you away. What is frightening you are all of the things like you not knowing your past; the children saying that you are different because you always shock them and other weird things. These are all deterrents to keep you from reaching your destiny. But you will never have a peace until you ignore it and stay focused.

"See the reason why Tertsrick became evil is because he wanted to be like the Great Spirit, even greater. When he was absorbed, not all of him was absorbed. Only his body. His spirit, which contained a portion of the Great Spirit, went into each person. Now each of them and everyone after them has a portion of the Great Spirit living inside. This way, the Spirit can communicate with us one-on-one. And it was the Great Spirit who called you to this place through you dreams.

"So if the Great Spirit is a part of all of us, why is there so much evil, you may wonder. The Great Spirit is a permissive spirit. It will allow you to do as you will, but there will be consequences for your actions. Likewise, the Great Spirit rewards you when you are good.

"This should answer the things you needed to know from this visit. It's time for you to return to your class now. Just remember to keep this a secret."

When that was said, Donovan immediately came out of his trance. And his hand dropped from the Door.

"How was it?" Mr. Peeker asked with a smile.

"Perfect, just like you said," Donovan answered and smiled back.

"Anyone else wants to touch the Door?" he asked. No one volunteered. When Donovan walked back to his group, he said to one of his friends, "Wow, I bet you thought I was going to stand there forever."

The friend said, "What do you mean, Don"? "You only touched it for a couple of seconds, then dropped your hand."

Donovan, again looking wide-eyed, quickly turned back and looked at Mr. Peeker. Mr. Peeker, still smiling, winked. And Donovan knew what that meant.

Everyone thanked Mr. Peeker for the interesting stories and headed out to meet up with the rest of the class. It was time to board the bus and go home. As they left the room, the guide stared at Donovan even though he was talking to the entire group. "You all had a good time?" he asked.

"Yes," everyone said except Donovan. He smiled and stared back. And the guide knew what that meant as well. He had nothing to say to Donovan from that point forward.

The two groups met up again and couldn't stop talking about their visit all the way back to the village. And when Donovan laid down that night, he said, "I'll see you later, Mr. Peeker, and thank you Great Spirit." With a smile, he peacefully went to sleep and slept calmly all night from that day forward.

HER NAME IS ANOI

*S*he's young, fair-skinned, and beautiful. Her hair is coiled and twisted up on top with a few strains hanging down her back. She is wearing a long, lacey cream-colored flowy sequin dress. It flutters as the breeze blows through the window. Her name is Reina, which means "queen" for she is heir to the throne.

It is early, just at the break of day. She is standing near an opened window, looking into a mirror and daydreaming about her day. Her heart's desire is coming to see her. He has asked to speak to her privately. She is excited. Maybe today, he will speak the words she wants to hear. Her father has made it known that he has what it takes to be a king.

Attending to her is her handmaid. She is younger than the princess and extremely attractive. Her skin is golden bronze and dewy. Her hair is also braided but twisted around her head. She is wearing a long mint-green-colored dress that accents her shape and highlights the innocence radiating from her face.

She and the princess are sisters by the father. The princess is the daughter of the queen. The maiden is the daughter of a concubine that father couldn't marry since her mother is not of royal blood.

A knock comes to the door. "Atrasnu, is that you?" the princess whispers.

"Yes," he replies.

She asks him to come in. He is a warrior and his physique tell of the battles he has endured. His sculpture is broad-shouldered with pumped arms. His midsection is toned, and his legs are built for running as well as for strength. He oversees the king's army, and he fights hard for he loves his country. His name is Atrasnu, which means gallant. He is desired by the princess to be her husband. The king has addressed him about marrying his daughter. But Atrasnu loves another. Her name is Anoi, which means desired one. And she is the princess' sister, and her handmaid.

"Your majesty," he says as he bows before her. "I need to speak to you of an important matter." She asks her handmaid to leave so that they can speak privately. He watches her as she leaves the room.

Slowly he turns to the princess and says, "Your father, the king, has spoken to me on several occasions. I'm sure that you are aware of this."

"Yes, I am aware, Atrasnu," she says. He takes her hand and asks, "May I speak freely, my princess?"

"Please do," she replies. She is blushing and full of anticipation.

"I love this land and I will do anything to defend it, to protect it, to whatever it takes to make sure that the kingdom lives forever. And I love your father. I desire to do nothing that would dishonor him. And, of course, I love you." She gasped.

"You are the beauty of the love your father shows for this great kingdom. You are the unattainable treasure to power and wealth that any man would hope to acquire. But, I, my princess, want more than money, power, and fame. I want what the heart wants."

When he said that, she shushes him and says, "Hush, my love. You don't have to say anymore. You speak with many flattering words. But they aren't needed here. I, too, want what the heart wants. Our union will not just be based on the earthly desires. It will be based on the deepest of hearts emotions. This, along with everything else, will not only make us the most powerful couple to have ever grace the land but the strongest because it will have a bond so deep that no one will be able to break it. For I love you, too."

Atrasnu, still holding her hand, drops to one knee. Her other hand covers her mouth as she believes he is about to propose. But Atrasnu says, "My princess, please wait patiently and let me continue. Please do not be angry with me. The last thing I want to do is to hurt you."

She says, "Angry, my love? How and why would I be angry with you?"

"My princess," he says as he stands. "I do not love you. I love another, your handmaid, Anoi. I have loved her from the moment I've laid eyes on her."

"That witch!" the princess says as she snatches her hand from him. "She has vexed you and caused you to love her. For she knew that you were mine, and she hates me because her mother is only a mistress."

"Reina, that is not it," he insisted.

"Then, what?" she questioned.

Pausing a little, he takes a deep breath. "You didn't hear me. You only heard her name. Again, I have loved her from the moment I saw her. She said nothing and did nothing to encourage it. It was me. At that time, I had no idea that you had any affection for me. So she nor I were trying to hurt you. I spoke to her one day as she was running errands. From that point on, our affections grew. One day, I went to your father to speak of her and he said he wanted to speak to me as well but about you. I tried to explain that I loved another, but he didn't want to hear it. He told me to forget her. I never told him who it was. I tried to do what he said, but I cannot. Like I said, the heart wants what the heart wants. I was coming to you to explain my situation and hoped that you would understand. I had no idea that you felt so deeply for me. I thought that you were just honoring your father's wishes. I thought that there was possibly someone else you truly loved. But now I realize that it is me." He dropped his head.

The princess, now not as mad but very hurt asks, "Why would you think that there would be someone else? You are the strongest, the most valiant, and the best looking. Shouldn't the future queen have the best? Even if I didn't love you, love has nothing to do with it. We are the best of all things. And those two things should be joined as one. If you have done as my father said and placed your affection on me, by now, you would be in love with me as I am with you."

"See, that is what I am talking about, my princess. You fell in love with me for what I look like and for what I am. If you would remove all these things from me, would you still feel the same?"

"That is ridiculous," she said. But then she thought within herself that maybe it isn't so ridiculous, after all. "Maybe that is what I will do—remove my handmade; yes, banish her. No, have her killed. And as for him, strip him of all his authority and wealth. When he sees how hard it is to live unprivileged, he will desire me! But I will have nothing to do with him. No one insults me that way. He will live out his life alone and poor."

She says to him, "You are correct, Atrasnu. I will remove those things from you. I will remove Anoi. She will be killed, and you will live as a pauper." She screams for the guards.

Anoi, listening through the door, rushes in. She stayed by the door because she knew the real reason Atrasnu came the visit. Atrasnu took Anoi by the hand and fled to the balcony. Down the trellis, they escaped.

The guards rushed in to find the princess crying. She yells for them to capture Atrasnu and Anoi for they have disgraced her. And she wanted someone to get the king.

The king comes in. They call him Stalwart for he is loyal, reliable, and hardworking. "What is the matter, my child?" he asks. "The guards summoned me with urgency."

"Father, father Atrasnu has disrespected me, and I want him tortured until he dies. Plus, he has ran off with Anoi. I hate her more, and I want her killed immediately. They don't deserve to live after what they have done to me," she replies.

"Calm down, my child, and tell me what they have done. Atrasnu has always shown great respect and honor to the crown and his country," the king says.

Through tears, she explains all that has taken place. The king holds his daughter as he listens. He comforts and ensures her that this matter will be dealt with. The king is influential all over, and he vows to contact his allies from the north, south, east, and west. There will be no place they can run to or hide and remain in peace. He will demand that they not be killed so that they can face the wrath of the throne. But the king too is hiding something from his daughter.

The king has an armor bearer who adores the princess. He is the son of a servant, a cook. His name is Paladin. He does not fight on the battlefield, but instead, makes sure nothing happens to the king while the king is at home. He even tastes his mother's food so that the king is never poisoned.

The king loves the young man and would rather see his daughter with him. He is a thin-framed man but robust. His archery is outstanding, and he can run like a gazelle. He prides himself on being quite the warrior. He desires to join the king's army but loves the king too much to leave him. Paladin has asked the king about the princess, but she is set on marrying Atrasnu. As the princess is talking, he is wondering how he can make everything work out for the best. Truthfully, the king loves Atrasnu and Anoi and doesn't want to see them harmed. But, right now, he cannot let the princess know any of this. After he left the princess' chamber, he summons Paladin. He needs to talk to him about possibly taking Atrasnu's place. But, most of all, he wants to discuss his feeling for his daughter.

As the king and Paladin talk, Atrasnu and Anoi run as fast and as far as they can. The land is divided into five sectors, one in the north, one in the south, one in the east, and one in the west, with the kingdom of Coridus being in the center.

Initially, the kingdom was one land where only humans with their pets and livestock lived. There was an abundance of wildlife as well. Everyone lived in harmony. The population grew at an enormous rate, causing people to spread far and wide. The farther they went from the kingdom, the less they felt that the king had control. They became self-centered and rebelled against what the kingdom initially stood for. For example, the king never wanted anyone to be overtaxed, overworked, or under-supplied with resources. This was because he never wanted his people to live stressed or in poverty. He always wanted them to be able to have family time, to attend community festivals and other social gatherings.

The king also felt that it was important to name the people with names that had a positive meaning. He believed that each time a person's name was spoken, it would release a power on them, and they would become what you called them. Many people believed this as well. As they migrated away from the kingdom, the ones who wanted to overpower others began to call them names like febrile-minded, hoping that this would break them down. If they could lessen some people, then they could control them and have them as slaves. Those people wanted to be revered as a king so that they too could be worshipped and served. This caused great tension among the people who expanded out.

When the king heard this, he was angry. He and his army went to rectify the problem. He hoped that he could reunited everyone without violence, but most of the time, that was not possible. He warred and warred. Many of those who had placed themselves in charged were killed in order to reestablish the land. Unfortunately, the king himself was slightly wounded during battle. This would later cause him to have serious consequences. But he was happy to regain control over all the land. Once again, the people were one. This king's name was Pravdo.

But the peace didn't last forever. Division came when the people started injecting animal blood into themselves.

~

When first reunited, everything seemed to go well. The people grew great in number again and this called for higher demands of everything. They were having a hard time meeting the needs of everyone and having time for the family too. So someone commented on how certain animals were extremely keen in areas where they needed help. Then they started thinking that if they injected animal blood into themselves, it may help them to do their jobs more efficiently. And the injections did enhance their senses and abilities. But it did something that they were not expecting. The people began to mutate. As they had children, their offspring were born mutated. This created a hybrid race. There were four types of blood injected: gorilla, dog, pig, and goat.

The people who injected gorilla's blood were people who needed great strength to perform their tasks, like lumberjacks. Plus, gorillas are great climbers and can exist off small amounts of food. This was a necessary attribute since many workers wandered long distances and food supply was always rationed. They called them Gorimen because most of them looked more like a gorilla than a human. As a group, they are the Gorimie.

The people who injected dog's blood were people who liked the way dogs were able to lead and guide. Dogs are also quick, loyal, protective, and bold fighters. Most of the people who injected dog's blood were military and herdsmen. People began to call them Canods because depending on how one nodded one's head, it would appear as though they were huge dogs for, they had little human features left. As a group, they are the Canodie.

The people who injected pig's blood were people who needed to be able to eat a lot of food and a variety of things without getting sick such as chefs and the king's tasters. Plus, pigs have a keener sense of smell than dogs. This attribute was desired by tasters because they could smell if someone were trying to poison the king. Chefs liked it because they could tell if the food was rotting. This way, merchants were not able to blend bad items with good ones. Farmers also liked it because they often blended their seeds to produce the best product. By having the pig blood in them, they could smell which seeds would produce the best flavors. They called these people the Pigramous because they had a bad habit of rumbling and sniffing through things, even if it didn't belong to them. And they left things very messy. As a group, they are called the Pigramie.

The people who injected goat's blood were people who needed endurance to cultivate landscapes. Landscapes could be very tough and rocky. In Coridus, the land varied all over. But there was one area that was far steeper and rockier than the rest. Cultivators realized that goats could scale and clear the land as they go. The tougher the territory, the better they are at leveling it off, making it viable for farming or whatever was needed. They are called the Naanunee because as they work, they make a soft naan sound like a goat. As a group, they are called the Naanunie.

So the kingdom became a kingdom of human and human-like. Each had annoying habits that began to irritate one another. When King Stalwart was officiated, he was young. And the hybrids had just about outnumbered the people. By the time he took over the kingdom, everyone was very much at odds. Even the hybrids were fighting against other hybrids. Some of the humans did not mind the hybrids, but quite a few did. The ones who minded wanted them to be destroyed. But King Stalwart did not feel that this was the right answer. So he, like his uncle before him, decided to divide the land and give each group of hybrids their own portion. And if the hybrids and the people would continue to help each other, they could live among their own kind. Some of the people wanted to live with the hybrids, and so they did. One group went north, one went south, one went east, and one went west. The king's territory remained at the center. That is why it was called Coridus, for it is the core and heart of the land.

Now the Canodie took the north because they adapted better to the colder climate. The Gorimie took the south because they liked the warmer climate. The Pigramie took the east because it was near most of the water, and water is needed for farming. The Naanunie took the west because the terrain was tougher. But some of all the hybrids remained in Coridus. King Stalwart valued all their attributes and used them effectively. So once again, everyone was at peace.

~

When King Pravdo was king, he was well-respected. Though he was a mighty warrior, he was kind. In many ways, the people were glad that the kingdom was reunited. Some of the region's leaders were cruel. King Pravdo took the weight and fear off the people. After they were reunited, they worked hard to keep peace. They had yearly ceremonies to honor him. They wanted to do the best, be the best for the best king ever. This is another reason why some started taking animal blood. They wanted to be able to perform better for the king.

In the beginning, they too were sorry that the hybrid effect occurred. But the king loved the people and felt that everyone could coexist. So when the people started complaining, he grew sad and his health began to decline more and more. The wound he obtained during battle was never quite right. And, eventually, he would die as a result. But not before he would anoint the person to take his place. This was Stalwart, and he was the king's nephew.

~

Though young, Stalwart had to step up for he was next in line to the throne.

He loved his uncle, family, and country. He did whatever he could to make them proud of him. Not too long after becoming king, he married because he knew how important it was for the kingdom to have an heir. He married a gorgeous thinned framed maiden. The two of them had grown up together. She was always a little on the weak side, but Stalwart knew that one day he would be king, so he told her not to worry. When he became king, she would have many assistants so she could rest to keep her strength. And this is what he did.

Soon after, he and the queen married, the queen became pregnant and bore a son. But it was weak and did not live long. King Stalwart assured her that things would be better the next time. About a year later, she bore him another child. This time it was strong and healthy, but it was a girl and the queen became weaker. King Stalwart, being a positive man, assured her again that things would be okay. But the queen knew differently. She told him that he had given her the best life that anyone could have offered her and that she loved him dearly. But for the rest of his life, he would have to go on without her. Even though he tried to say no, she wouldn't hear of it. Later that night, she died. King Stalwart loved her so much, he vowed within himself to never remarry. He took several concubines instead. He hoped that his daughter would inherit the throne, though this was not practiced at that time. And he decided that if the kingdom wouldn't hear of that, then let someone else rule. He had done all that he felt he could do regarding the matter.

As his daughter grew, she was amazingly beautiful like the queen but strong like the king. The king could see nothing but the queen each time he looked at her. This made him very weak for his daughter and her demands. And from a young age, she admired a lad who was the son of her father's younger brother. He loved to fight and vowed to be in the king's army. He loved his family, and his kingdom, and he wanted to protect it. The princess knew of this and admired him even more. Plus, he was astonishingly handsome. She knew he would make the perfect husband. This was Atrasnu.

Unfortunately, things didn't always turn out the way she wanted them to. Just like the people who initially took the animal blood, they never thought that they would metamorphose into a hybrid. And the princess never thought that any man would prefer another woman over her. But that is exactly what happened. And because of this, he and the woman feared for their lives. So they ran.

~

Atrasnu and Anoi first went east to the land of Pigonia, but it used to be called Fittonia before it was reunited with Coridus. It was called that because it was fertile with all types of plants and odd vegetation. It was discovered that many of the plants were great for medicinal purposes, but some were poisonous. And they had to be careful because they looked very similar to each other. Yet even the poisonous plants could be used for a good cause. This was another reason why the Pigramie went to that area. They were great at distinguishing one plant from another.

But Atrasnu chose to go there because that is where his family lived before he was born. But when all the trouble initially broke out, his family moved back to Coridus for safety. Even though the Pigramie now populated that area, he felt that it would be a good place to live for it always had plenty of fresh water, and it was a place of beauty.

The quickest way to get there was to go by the riverbank. But they didn't, in fear of being easily seen, they crept among the dense forest. By the time they reached the village, the king had already notified the Pigramie. And they were waiting for them. Even though King Stalwart had made the hybrids agree to remain in peace, the people had come under a cruel authority. The king had no idea of how brutal the leader was. They kept the king unaware on purpose.

Being that the Pigramie were greedy and ate quite frequently, they made the villagers work all the time to ensure that there was enough food. If not, then the Pigramie would begin to eat the people. This left the people in constant fear. For the effects of the blood not only made the people look like animals, they acted like them. Pigonia began to look dirty as well because the Pigramie were slobs.

Now King Stalwart, like his uncle before him, wanted everyone to be kind. He was good and did not tolerate evil except when it came to his daughter. Being that she was his weakness, he bended to her rants and raves. He would set aside his values for her then secretly compensate anyone who was offended by her outbursts. He loved everyone and everything. He did what he could to keep peace though out the land.

When the king had asked the leader of the Pigramie, Boardash, to capture Atrasnu and Anoi, he was to return them unharmed. But Boardash had his own plans. He had seen a picture of Atrasnu and Anoi and desired Anoi for himself.

Boardash looked like a pig, short and extremely fat. He wanted to be more human and handsome, like Atrasnu. So he planned to inject Atrasnu's blood into himself and to breed Anoi. By breeding Anoi, their children would have more human features. Therefore, he ordered his army to capture them but to tell the king that they never arrived. The people, out of fear, would do whatever they were told. They were even too frightened to leave, fearful for their family members. They knew for certain that Boardash would hurt them if they told what was going on. He would hurt them if he even thought they had told someone. He was extremely paranoid. And if the king found out, he would lie and sweet talk him into returning them. But the people knew what the outcome would be if they had to go back.

As for Boardash, he was not only dishonest to the king, he was also dishonest to his own kind. He spoke greatly of turning all his inhabitants into a Pigramous, but this wasn't true. He knew that many humans began to detest the Pigramie. He felt that it was their appearance they hated. That weighed heavily on him, therefore, he wanted to be more human. Once he saw that the blood was working, he was going to tell the other Pigramie to drink a potion that would make them stronger. But it would kill them, for he also feared being overthrown by one of his own kind. He did not believe someone with only human blood could overtake him, but he wasn't sure about his own kind. Therefore, he didn't want all the pig blood removed.

He was especially afraid of his brother, who had always resented him for becoming the leader. That resentment tormented him as well. Therefore, he did not rest well. He was already edgy and angry. This, and the fact that he was loath his own appearance, also made him extremely violent.

Atrasnu was a prayer warrior as well. He believed that this is what gave him his advantage over the enemy. So when he and Anoi came to the edge of the forest, at the beginning of the farm and grasslands, he stopped to pray. He said, "Creator of all things, bless Anoi and me. Keep us safe and give us a place to live in peace and we will be forever grateful." Anoi did not say anything after he prayed. She didn't believe in prayer. Her mother used to pray all the time, but things never seemed to change. Life was always hard for them both. The last prayer she said was when she asked for her mother to live. She didn't, so Anoi stopped praying.

As soon as they stepped onto the grassland, Atrasnu could tell that something was wrong. It was strangely quiet. Then, out from behind huge stalks and other barriers, came the Pigramie dressed in battle armor. They charged with swords and slings. Atrasnu, who never left without his defensive gear, drew as well. Anoi stayed close behind.

With two swords drawn, Atrasnu began to fight. One of the Pigramie grabbed Anoi, but she was not without her weapons. Tucked in her hair, she kept sharp, long pins.

She stabbed the Pigramous in the main artery of his neck, injuring him so badly that he had to let her go. He tried to run away, but he was bleeding profusely. Then, he dropped to his knees and died. Anoi rushed to help Atrasnu fight. He had been slightly cut on the arm but did his best to maintain focus so he could try to fight his way out.

In the back of him, Atrasnu could hear more rustling noises. He was growing weary because he thought another set of Pigramie was coming. Yet, to his surprise, the noise was being made by people and Pigramie who wanted peace. All of the Pigramie were not like Boardash.

A couple of people carried Anoi to safety while the rest fought tirelessly until they could get the battle under control. The few Pigramie that were left fled when they realized that there was no way that they could win. Tired and exhausted, Atrasnu asked why all of this happened. They explained that King Stalwart had sent word for their leader, Boardash, to keep watch just in case he and Anoi had arrived. King Stalwart wanted them captured so he could talk about what happened with the princess. "But Boardash had his own ideas. He wanted you dead because he wanted Anoi for himself. Some of us who were not happy with Boardash decided to thwart his plans and help you fight. So we sent our own spies to tell us if and when you arrived. We decided that if you did come this way, it was our signal that it was time to do away with our brutish leader. While over half of the Pigramie were away, we overtook Boardash, the others and killed them. Then we came to help you defeat his army. We are not worried about the few who got away. We have enough people in the village waiting to subdue them. Unfortunately, they will have to be put to death as well. We cannot take a chance on any rebellion".

"The king was right. It is better to strive to live in peace. Since not all of the Pigramie are evil, we wanted to live as King Stalwart said. So we felt that this was a good opportunity to take over and start again. We know that we will have to settle this with the king somehow, but that is our problem. Boardash was extremely evil. And he was getting worse by the day. Something had to be done. As for you and Anoi, it is still not safe here. And we do not want to have to tell the king that we have seen you. So be gone, our friends, and we pray that things will work well for you somewhere else."

The people placed a balm made of herbs on Atrasnu's wound. It healed immediately. They gave him the rest in case he would need it later. So after some much-needed rest and food, Atrasnu and Anoi left to go northwest. They thanked their newfound friends, and Atrasnu promised that if he could ever help them, he would.

As he and Anoi traveled, he figured that the king had spread word all over. Therefore, he wasn't sure that his presence would be accepted anywhere. But he would take that chance. If he and Anoi had to return to the kingdom or die, it would not be without a fight. He and she both agreed, there is no better reason to fight than to fight for love.

As they traveled, Atrasnu had a chance to admire the beauty of the land. He really wished that he could camp right where they were, somewhere in between regions, among the trees. But he thought that if he did, he would have to worry about more than one region attacking him. He believed that the two of them could eat off the land, but when they needed water or supplies, this would pose a problem, so they trampled on as quietly as they possibly could.

~

After a while, the air began to turn crisp. The coldness was a sign that they were nearing the land of the Canodie. Atrasnu knew that they had to be extremely careful. Though they had a good since of smell, they had an even better since of hearing. They could hear miles beyond their territory. Still, he was hopeful. Many of them used to be a part of the king's army, and he had hoped that they would have sympathy on their situation. He and Anoi would soon find out.

From a distance, they saw a row of what looked like scarecrows. But Atrasnu knew better. Many of the Canodie were tall with very thin legs. As they stood, their legs together looked like poles. And Atrasnu knew that if they wanted to attack, it wouldn't take long for them to reach he and Anoi.

The Canodie had another great advantage. They could run on all four extremities, which gave them great speed.

Knowing that they had been spotted, he and Anoi stood very still but prepared for a fight. Yet, being that they had not attacked them while they were resting was a good sign.

All at once, the Canodie lifted their spears. Three of them stepped forward. Out of the three, one stepped out even farther. "Atrasnu, my old friend. "Come forth, you and Anoi," he howled. This gave he and Anoi some peace, but their spears were still drawn. So they did not do as they were summonsed. Atrasnu came close, but Anoi waited in the brush as Atrasnu had instructed her.

Again, he yelled, "Atrasnu, my old friend. Come closer so I can talk to you. This is Smurnoff. You remember me, don't you? We used to play fight together as kids. And we both desired to serve in the king's army." Doing as he was asked to do, Atrasnu approached with caution.

"Yes, of course, I remember you. How could I forget. I was sorry to see you move away. I had hoped that you would have stayed in Coridus with the king," Atrasnu replied.

"Yes, that was a hard decision to make. My wife wanted to be around more people like us. So we left. But my heart is still to the king. He has always been extremely kind to us. And loyalty deserves loyalty. Not only that, the people love me here. They love me so much that they made me their leader. I am good to all, hybrid and human. I am just like the king. Speaking of loyalty, Atrasnu, you do not seem very loyal to me," he said.

"Why do you say that, Smurnoff?" Atrasnu asked.

"Well, for one, you are out here. Why are you so far away from your post? This is a long way off from Coridus. What, have you decided to live with us instead?" As Smurnoff spoke, the other Canodie snickered.

"May I speak truths with you Smurnoff?" Atrasnu asked.

"Yes, of course, my old friend," he replied.

With one hand lifted to swear by, and his head bowed to honor him, Atrasnu said, "I love the king and I love my country. In no way will I ever stop being true to them. But there may come a time when one has to be true to oneself, and it may differ from what someone else says."

Smurnoff interrupts and says, "I don't understand, my old friend. My thoughts are my people's thoughts, which are also the king's thoughts. Everyone should think the same thing. If not, then something is broken. That something is loyalty. So, again, I ask you, have you broken your loyalty to the king, Atrasnu?"

As Smurnoff is speaking, the Canodie snarl.

Atrasnu can't tell if the situation is turning against his favor, so he prays within himself for wisdom. Then, he answers and says, "Yes, I agree." He then flatters Smurnoff, saying, "Smurnoff, I honor you as I honor the king when I speak to you. You are the leader of your region; therefore, you are the king of your territory, and you are great. You deserve the respect of a king. But my situation is like your situation when you decided to move. You desired to be with the king, but your family desired differently. However, you still maintain the king's rules but just in a different place. I honor him as well, but the princess demanded that I should marry her. I tried to reason with her, but she would not hear of it. I wanted to stay and present myself before the king for his final say on the matter, but the princess was hysterical. So, until I could find a way to discuss it with the king rationally, I ran. I came this way because I knew that we had a great rapport, hoping that your people would allow me to rest for a while. And now that I know that you are their leader, maybe you can help me speak to the king." Atrasnu knew that this was not all true, but he had to keep things calm. "Forgive me, Great One, for lying", he said to himself.

Smurnoff nodded and said, "Yes, I see your dilemma. But I, too, have a dilemma. The king has asked me to seize you if you come this way and bring you back immediately. So you cannot rest here. And what you said about the princess is true. She has paid us to kill Anoi. Her words are like the king's words. And since the king has not mentioned anything about Anoi, I must do as the princess says."

Upon hearing that Anoi could not go free unharmed, Atrasnu lifted his head and slowly lowered his hand. Then wisdom came to him, and he said, "Tell me, Smurnoff, what would you do if the king had told you that you could leave his army and the princess got upset and ordered to have your family killed for making you go? How would you have honored that situation, my old friend? Would you have stayed to save your family or would have done what you needed to do to reason with the king, knowing the whole time your family may not be safe?"

Now all the Canodie were looking at each other puzzled. Smurnoff too took time before he responded. "Yes, my friend, I see your situation. So tell me, how can we settle this and still remain loyal to the king?"

Atrasnu answered by saying, "Smurnoff, your people were right to make you their leader. You are wise and just. As I said before, I honor you as I honor the king. What I would do if I were in your situation is to trust what I am about to say. We have always trusted each other in the past, and there is no reason for you not to trust me now. You have not seen Anoi, but I know that you know she is with me. What I will do is that I will make you a promise that I will return to face the king on my own. And I will take Anoi with me. I will let you watch me leave and go toward Coridus. That way, if the king acquires further, you can tell him that you saw me afar off and that I was already traveling in the direction of the kingdom. Therefore, there was no need to assist me. As far as Anoi, you did not see her. And that is all I would say. This way you would not be lying, and I will have another chance to resolve the situation."

Smurnoff, pleased and flattered with that response, said, "Why, yes, that is exactly what I will do. Yes, we all should try to live together peacefully. That is what the King would want, and that is exactly what I will do. Go, walk toward Coridus, my old friend. Then my army and I will turn our backs and Anoi can catch up to you. Go in peace, my old friend."

Atrasnu again bowed before him saying, "Like the king, you are worthy of honor. May you live long and prosper in all that you do. And if there is ever anything, I can do for you, I will my, old friend. I will."

They did exactly as they discussed. Once far out of sight and Anoi again by his side, they let out a sigh of relief. They took some time to sit and talk for a moment.

"What are we going to do?" Anoi asked. "We can't go back to Coridus, and I'm too afraid to go anywhere else. Maybe you should have let them kill me. That way, you could go back to the princess and live in peace. She may be mad at you, but I'm sure she won't stay angry for long. She loves you, and most of all, she loves having her way. She will enjoy knowing that I am dead. And if you beg for her forgiveness, she will love that too." Anoi burst into tears.

Atrasnu holds and comforts her by saying, "No, we are in this together. If you die, I die. There is no life without you. I know it will take longer now since we are having to back-track, but we will still attempt to go to the west. When the Naanunie lived in Coridus, the king had the most trouble with them. Maybe they will ignore the king's request and let us live in peace."

~

After some time in the forest, Anoi says, "We have had such success here. No one has bothered us. Let's make our lives here, away from everyone."

"I wish we could do that. But, soon our necessary supplies will run out, and we will have to get close to someone's land to replenish. Until we make peace with someone, we will never live free," Atrasnu replies.

"I'm tired of worrying, Atrasnu. Look at the wear and tear on our hands. I see the stress breaking down the youth of your face. I feel the youth of mine leaving," she says.

"I know. I don't know how, but I still believe that somehow things will work out. But for certain, we cannot stay here. I'm sure that the Canodie will visit Coridus at some time, and they will find out that we never arrived. For that reason, Smurnoff will know that I tricked him. And, surely, he will come looking for us. He will want to know if we are dead or hiding," he responds.

"Well, if he won't stop until he finds us, then why are we going to live with the Naanunie?" Anoi asked.

"The Naanunie are an extremely stubborn group. That is why they had so much trouble with other hybrids. They could deal with people better. They are not particularly fond of the Canodie because they like to tell others what to do. So, if I can convince them to let us stay, they would not care what the others thought. And there is a strong agreement among the hybrids. They respect each other's territory," he says. This seemed to renew her hope.

Once again, they packed up and started on their journey. After a long while, they came to the edge of the forest. The plains were well manicured and bountifully orchard with all types of trees and vegetation. A sweet aroma from the cleanliness of the land, and its fruits and plants, filled the air. Atrasnu looked at Anoi and she back at him, both smiling. They felt that this would be a wonderful place to reside. Hand in hand, they walked toward the village of the Naanunie.

~

It was very early in the morning when the two of them arrived in the camp. But the Naanunie are hard workers. So they were already up and stirring about. Atrasnu asked a local where was the leader. He desired to talk to him. When the local looked up, he pointed, staring in the direction of where he could be found. "What is his name?" Atrasnu inquired.

"He is a she. And we call her Mira, for she is beautiful to look at," the local said.

Atrasnu thanked the local as he walked toward the leader's dwelling. When he looked back, he saw the local still staring. Then he also noticed that others had stopped and stared as they went by. Anoi noticed it as well and commented, "I'm beginning to feel a little unsure, Atrasnu. Do you still want to continue?"

"Yes. No one has sounded any type of alarm, and no one is trying to subdue us. We have come this far. Let's see what is going to happen," he answered.

When they arrived at the door, there was a Naanunee on one side and a human on the other side. The human grabbed Anoi and began to examine her briskly. Atrasnu ran to her defense, but the Naanunee detained him. "Calm down," he demanded.

"What is the meaning of this?" Atrasnu asked. "We have just come to inquire of your leader. We do not mean anyone any harm," he insisted.

Again, the Naanunee said to calm down. A few seconds later, the human let Anoi go. He looked at the Naanunee and shook his head. The Naanunee asked what they wanted to talk to the leader about. Atrasnu told him that he and his wife wanted a place to stay and that they loved the way the Naanunie kept their land. They wanted to live among an environment like that. Then, the Naanunee asked for their names so that he could announce them to the leader. Atrasnu felt that since they were not arrested or attacked, that the two at the door did not know who they were. But, to be on the safe side, he gave him a false name. He said that their names were Sretfrid, Mr. and Mrs. Sretfrid.

The human went in and stayed for a few minutes. When he came out, he said it was okay to approach the leader. Atrasnu let Anoi go in first so that he could make sure neither of the doormen grabbed her.

~

The inside was even more beautiful than the outside land and the resident's dwellings. The hallway that they had to walk up led to another set of doors. As they approached the doors, they automatically opened. Not only were the Naanunie neat, they were very innovative. Once through the doors, there were two other doormen, but this time, they were female—one human and one Naanunee. They pointed straight ahead to another set of doors. Atrasnu said to himself, "No wonder it took the outside guard so long to return." It was a long walk. But this didn't matter to them, especially if this walk led to their freedom.

The next set of doors led to a room even more elegant than before. This time, there were guards all around the room, not just at the door. In front of them was a stage about five to six steps high with five chairs on it. The chair in the middle was the largest, and there sat a woman who asked them to come closer. She was still somewhat far away, and they could not see her face clearly. But from what they could tell, she seemed to be beautiful just as the local said.

This time, Atrasnu and Anoi walked side by side to the woman. As they got close, they could not believe their eyes. They now knew why the residents stared as they went by. The leader looked like Anoi except for a few goat-like characteristics, which were her hands and ears. They would not have even noticed the ears if her hair was down. But it was up and wrapped like Anoi's.

When the leader spoke, her words made a sound like a goat. "Well, I see that it is true what my guard has said, Mrs. Sretfrid. You favor me a lot, like I could be your daughter." Anoi was a bit puzzled by the leader's choice of words. She did not see where she was too much older than the leader.

"So, you want to live here among us, is that correct?", she asked.

"Yes," Atrasnu said, and Anoi nodded.

"Well, let's discuss that over a meal. I never like to make decisions on an empty stomach, and I was just about to eat when you arrived." The Naanunie ate often as well. But they were basically vegetarians. She went on to say, "You look like you could use a bath and a rest. I will assign you a chambermaid who will show you where you can get cleaned up and put your things down."

Atrasnu and Anoi were pleased to hear this and followed the maiden to their room.

The maiden is a young human girl. She stared at Anoi a lot, too, but not like the others, more like she was trying to warn her. Anoi noticing this and decided to make light conversation with her. She didn't want to frighten her or give her cause to say something to the leader. So she said, "Yes, it is amazing how we look so much alike. Who is her mother and father?"

The girl, making sure everything is okay, looks at Anoi and says, "Her mother is dead, and her father does not live in the village." As she leaves the room, she signals her eyes toward the window. Anoi notices but does not say anything. She thanked the girl for making sure everything was okay.

After the girl left, she walks over to the window and sees writing in the dust. It said, "Be careful. They see and hear more."

Not to bring attention to what she read, she goes to Atrasnu and says, "I think this is going to work out here. She hugs him, then whispers "window" in his ear. As she lets go of him, she smiles and nods.

Atrasnu, catching on, says, "Yes, I think you are right." He walks to the window and sees for himself. After reading what was written, he takes his hand and wipes it away, saying, "Isn't the woodwork beautiful?"

"Yes, it most certainly is," Anoi replies.

They realize something is up, and they must be careful. By accident, Atrasnu moves the drapes back just a little. When he goes to close it because the sun is so bright, he notices that there are bars on the window. Then, he notices that there aren't any mirrors. He also felt that this was strange.

Suddenly, someone knocks on the door. This startles them because they don't know if someone was watching and figured out what they were doing. But it was the maiden again bringing them fresh clothing. She says that the leader prefers for them to dress in their attire and to hurry because she is hungry.

Atrasnu asks the maiden why there aren't any mirrors. He said he wanted to shave. But the maiden said that the leaders don't like anyone to stare in a mirror. She and she alone is the only one who should be admired. The maiden looks down and says "Hurry," and walks out. They looked at each other, and they quickly wash and get dressed.

By the time the maiden returned, they had just finished getting ready. She escorted them to a room where the leader and others were seated at a table along with servants standing holding dishes of food and vessels of drinks. The leader asked them to sit, and the servants came to each of them, one by one, placing food on their plates. Once everyone was served, the servants left the room. Then the leader said, "Enjoy," and they all began to eat.

The food was exceptionally good, so good that no one hardly talked while they ate. Everyone ate with haste and so did Atrasnu and Anoi. They were extremely hungry but were too afraid to show it. Then the leader clapped her hands and the servants came back in again. This time, with all type of fruits, baked breads, jellies, and candies. Again, they plowed into it like it was their first meal or their last.

After letting out several belches, the leader clicked her glass and said, "Now, let's talk. Why do you want to live with us? And where do you come from, Mr. and Mrs. Sretfrid?"

Atrasnu began to speak, but she silenced him. "I would prefer to hear from your wife."

Anoi said, "We come from Coridus. We have heard about the beauty of this place and decided that it would be a nice place to live and a nice place to start a family."

"Start a family", the leader replied. And then she laughed out loud. All sitting at the table began to chuckle too. Atrasnu and Anoi did not see what was funny but smiled to keep everyone at ease.

"I see," she continued. "Well, Mrs. Sretfrid, I seem to have one little problem with that." When she said that, they knew that there would be trouble. And neither Atrasnu nor Anoi had anything on them to fight with. They were at the mercy of those who were at the table.

"The problem that I have is that some time ago, a man from Coridus came here with a picture of two people the king wanted brought back to the kingdom. It is strange because the pictures looked very much like you two, but the names were different. Because of this, I feel that you two are lying to me. You are actually Atrasnu and Anoi, is that correct? she asked.

There was nothing that they could do at this point but to try to remain calm. They replied, "Yes."

"So, tell me, why did you try to deceived me?" she asked.

Again, Atrasnu went to respond but she only wanted to hear from Anoi. "Well, we were afraid, your greatness. We had hoped that the demand had not come this far, and we just wanted to live in peace. We have done nothing to the king. Anoi continued until she had fully explained the situation."

After she was finished, the leader said, "I allowed you to come in because I do not care what the king says. I have my personal issues with him. But I also allowed you to come in because when I looked at your picture, you looked so much like me that I had to see you for myself. Of course, the picture of you is much younger, but I can still see that it is you."

When Atrasnu and Anoi heard that she did not care for the king, they felt that they had a chance to remain there in peace. They were hoping that she understood their position and would forgive them for lying.

The leader continued, "But, to be truthful, I am still not pleased with you, Anoi, or you, Atrasnu."

Both are on edge again.

"I am not pleased with you, Atrasnu, because you worked close with the Canodie. They have always been a thorn in my side. I deal with them on a small basis. But they and you are good friends. I don't like anyone who is good friends with the Canodie. You are very handsome, and I see why the princess wanted you for herself. I may have some use for you because I have not yet chosen a mate. Plus, I would love to have what the princess could not have. It would please me and totally infuriate her. But, as for you, Anoi, I have even a greater dislike for you. And I'm sure you have no idea why. It is not because we look so much alike even though that does make matters worse. It is that you, me, and the princess are sisters by your father, the king. Now do you see why we favor so much? My mother was part Naanunee and one of the king's concubines like your mother. When she was young, her features were light, more human-like. The king impregnated her, but as she grew in pregnancy, her features became more like a Naanunee. They were so strong that the king did not want anything else to do with her. When he allowed us to have our own land, my mother left with me. He saw that my little hands were like my mother's, and he feared that I would turn out like her. Therefore, he didn't care if I stayed or not.

My mother loved him, far more that the queen or the other women. It broke her heart when he thought that she would be better off with her own kind and that I would be too. She was sickly all of my life, and when I was at fourteen years old, she died. But I did get most of my father's attributes. I am a warrior like him, and I have proven myself from time to time.

A few years back, I became the leader of these great people. For you to stay would be a problem for me. But I decided as I ate that I would be more merciful to you than my father was to my mother since it is not your fault. You can stay as a worker. You can wash my clothes. Yes, that is what you can do. You can wash my staff's clothes, too. Now I will have one sister as my servant and the love of my other sister. And this will please me well."

Before Atrasnu and Anoi could take in all that she said, Mira yelled, "Away with them until I am ready for them."

The guards rushed to each and took them away to a room that had four doors with bars at the windows. Atrasnu was placed in one and Anoi was placed in another. In each room was a cot, and a pipe coming from the wall with a slow stream of water flowing into a gridded hole, which could be used as a commode. There was no light in the cells. The light came from a small barred window. When the sun went down, that entire area was dark. The only other light was from a single bulb that hung in the hallway between the cells. The cell doors also had a slot for food.

Atrasnu sat with his head in his hands as he listened to Anoi cry. He calls out to her, "Anoi, I will always love you. Even if I must marry Mira, I will somehow find a way to ease your burden until I can get you somewhere safe."

Anoi says, "You should have let me die."

Hurt by her words, Atrasnu begins to pray. He says, "Creator of all things, I'm sorry for not seeking you before we came here. Please don't be angry with me. I have tried to do good in all things. No one can be as good as You. But what have I done to deserve such great pain and distress? I meant no harm to anyone. I just wanted to love freely. If what I have done has been so bad, then let me and me alone suffer. Anoi only followed me. Let me take her pain. But if what I have fought for is good in Your sight, then somehow bring good to all of this. Help me, Great One, help me." Atrasnu continued to listen to Anoi crying until she fell asleep.

Later that evening, about nine, the maiden came in to give them soap, tissue, and a cup. She slipped it through the opening in the door. Atrasnu got a larger portion because the leader liked him. But on his tissue was a note. It said, "I will be back within an hour. Be ready." So Atrasnu disposed of the note down the hole that the water ran in.

About thirty minutes later, the maiden came back. This time she opened Atrasnu's door and told him to hurry. You must leave now. She then went to Anoi's doors and opened it. "Get her, and stay quiet. We don't have much time."

Atrasnu did just that. Anoi wanted to be left alone because she felt that she was doomed wherever she went. But Atrasnu hushed her, picked her up and followed the maiden.

They slowly crept passed the guards who were sleeping and exited by the back way. Atrasnu thanked her and asked why were the guards sleeping so hard? She told him that she had put something in their drink to make them rest. She also said that they have a hard time staying awake past nine o'clock because everyone is used to getting up around four in the morning. She just made it so they wouldn't be startled when they went passed. She also said that they would know it was her who let them go, so she was planning on going with them. She felt that she could be a good help because she knew the Naanunie well. She also wanted to leave because Mira had her father killed so that she could be the leader. Mira made her maiden to keep an eye on her because she feared she would revenge her father's death. But she had overheard Mira saying that she planned on killing her because she didn't trust her. So releasing them would help her as well.

By that time, Anoi got herself together and they all fled deep into the forest.

They kept going until they were far out of reach. Not sure what to do, they sat down to rest for a while. Then the maiden saw a cave, and they decided to check it out. Once in the cave, they heard some noise that sounded like rain. As they walked deeper and deeper, the ground became soft. Somehow, water was getting in but how and from where they did not know. After an hour or so, they saw a bright light shining. It looked as though there was another way into the cave. When they had reached the opening, it was an opening on the side of a mountain, many miles high up behind a waterfall. They were elated because they would not have to go near the villages for fresh water. They decided to live the rest of their days in the cave. Atrasnu asked the young girl what her name was. She said that her name was Charity. Atrasnu said that her name fit her because she was merciful to them from the beginning. And the chance she took was an act of love. But he decided to call her Felicity, for she had brought them fortune and much happiness.

All was peaceful for quite some time, until early one morning, they heard rumbling coming their way. And before they could get their weapons, what seemed like men were standing over them. They were Gorimen. The leader spoke and said, "Be still, and fear not."

"My name is Calamus, and we are not here to hurt you. With me is my wife, Acorus, and my son, Vale. Many think that we are a cruel race, but it is not true. We are gentle but protective of our own. We visit this part of the forest often and have watched you go back and forth through the trees. This time when we saw that you were staying, our leader, Ogon sent us to speak to you. He knows why you have traveled back and forth through the trees. He knows that the king had summoned you to the kingdom. But that has been a long time ago. He decreed years ago that he wanted you to live free wherever you were. He sent his army to find you, but they were unable to locate you. He wanted you to know that he was able to settle the matter with the princess. She fell in love with the king's armorbearer, Paladin. They married and have several children, four who are male. There is an heir to the throne, and the eldest son became king last year.

Then, a great sickness came through the land and the king along with his daughter and her husband succumbed to the disease. But the king made it clear that you would always be welcomed. The princess had hoped to see you again as well. She was sorry for the things she said and did. If you return to the kingdom, you will be clothed and housed in the king's house. They refer to you both as their missing family, an aunt and an uncle to the king's heirs."

Atrasnu and Anoi now realized why their faces looked so worn. At first, they thought it was from the stress that they had been under. But now, they know that it had been years since they left. Far more years than they had thought. They were now old. The maiden could tell what they were thinking as they looked at each other. She nodded her head. She said, "This is true. My leader was supposed to tell you to come home, but she refused. This is also why she would not follow you. She feared what would happen if you told. Also, they laughed at you when you said you were going to have children because they saw you as beyond those years. I came along because I wanted to be your daughter since I no longer had any family."

Calamus went on to say, "Now that the king is gone, I will share this with you. It has been passed down from my ancestors. The king and his uncle before him had a secret. They did not want to get rid of the hybrids because they both injected a little bit of each types of blood in them. They did this so that no one race would have an advantage over them and that they would be able to relate to all kinds. But they didn't inject enough to change. Just enough to develop the instinct. So they both felt that each group were just as much a part of them as the humans were. This is what made them such good leaders. And the king encouraged his grandsons to do the same. He wanted them to have a love for all creations."

After everything was said, the Gorimie helped them up. They all hugged, and Atrasnu and Anoi cried. The Gorimie gave them horses to ride back to the kingdom. And when they returned, the entire kingdom rejoiced. Neither Atrasnu nor Anoi told of all their travail. Everyone wanted to let bygones be bygones. Atrasnu and Anoi formally married, and Felicity-Charity became their child. They got everything Atrasnu prayed and fought hard for, just not in the way that they imagined. Anoi now realized that prayer does work, so she started praying again. Felicity-Charity married and had several children. Atrasnu and Anoi lived for many years, and they couldn't have been happier if they had tried.

AND WITH A FLASH

I t was early in the morning. Kyra couldn't sleep. She didn't know why. She just couldn't. It wasn't too muggy. It was what some would consider to be a perfect night. But something was bothering her. So she wrestled for a while before she decided to get up and walk around. She got a cup of tea, sat at the table, and thought about some things. Then she thought she heard something. Something strange and out of place. "What is that?" she said. It sounded like it was coming from outside, so she got up to look out of her living room window.

Mason is on his way home from a late-night party. He had a little too much to drink, so he was driving slowly. He didn't want to drive too slow because he did not want it to seem obvious that something was wrong. And he didn't want to drive too fast because he needed to maintain control. He thought about pulling over, but his wife had been complaining about him staying out all night. Therefore, he wanted to get home before she had a tantrum. Then, he saw flashing lights behind him approaching fast. He just knew he was busted because he couldn't fake his condition. He slowly pulls over, turns off the ignition, rolls down the window, and lays his head on the steering wheel. Before the lights could reach him, he had passed out cold.

~

Thomas is working the overnight shift at the local radio station. He is having a lot of problems working the equipment. He believed that a predicted storm was causing some disturbances. And he is tired of the old equipment. He has been to the council many times requesting them to modernize. They said that it is on the agenda, but there are a few things that must be done first. He loves his job and always knew that radio was in his destiny. He wanted to move to a big city and become a major radio host. But when his father died young, that only left him and his mother. He loves his mother dearly and wants to make sure she is well taken care of. Therefore, he decided that he would not move. He, his wife and young child, all live with his mother. The wife is not particularly fond of looking after her. And this causes a little tension between him and her. To help alleviate the situation, he works at night while his mother is sleeping. His son loves his grammy, and if she calls out at night, he jumps up to help. The wife only gets up if she has to. And when she does, she makes it known that she is not happy.

~

Tammy and Jake are sheriff deputies, working the night shift, and they are out on patrol. Nothing much is happening tonight, and they are glad because just a few nights ago, they were on watch for a couple of escapees. They were thought to be heading in the direction of the town, but no one has seen anything. The search was lowered from a high-visual to a low keep-an-eye-out awareness. The two of them are talking and laughing over some things that are going on in the office as they patrol the town. After a lap or two, they decide to walk and flash their lights just to make sure everything is okay. As they walk, Tammy thinks it is too quiet. Jake wonders why because everything is basically closed at this time of night. Tammy agrees but usually as they walk past the mayor's house, his dogs bark. This time they didn't. "Maybe they are inside," Jake said. "Maybe so," Tammy responded. "But just to make sure, let's just check his house out." Jake agreed, and together they walked back.

When they arrived, they flashed their lights to see if anything seemed out of place. Nothing stood out, so they went around to the side where the dogs were, and they could see their eyes glowing in the dark. When they flashed their lights to get a closer look, the dogs were hoovering under the side porch, snarling but not aggressively barking like they usually do.

Tammy said, "That's strange."

Jake replied, "Yeah, I know. Like something has spooked them."

But then, they noticed that the dogs weren't quite looking at them. As they started to turn around, something wet and sticky was thrown at them. It hit them directly in their faces. They dropped their flashlights to try to remove whatever it was. But it was over whelming, and it caused them to lose their breath. They passed out and fell to the ground.

~

Thomas is rapping things up. It is almost time for him to go home. The local radio station goes off at 2 a.m. The airway is then maintained by the law enforcement. They also play music but come on from time to time just to give a quick weather report and an everything-seems-fine tonight message. Unfortunately, an occasional alert goes out as well.

Tonight, Thomas is ready to go home. He is working a seven-day stretch this week because the other night person is not feeling well. The love he has for broadcasting helps keep him from feeling pressured, and the fact that it allows him to have a break from his wife's complaining.

He's not sure as to what happened between the two of them. He believes that she was disappointed when he did not leave for the big city. He feels that she didn't want to be a stay-at-home mom nor a caretaker for the elderly. He also believes that she was hyped on the fame and fortune that she thought a big city career would offer because every time he talked about his dreams, she lit up. Now she slams things and finds excuses to leave the house. It is very disheartening for him to admit that the house is more at peace when she is not there. He really wishes that things could be different, but he doesn't know what else to do. Even though he doesn't go to church, he spoke to the local pastor. He told him to pray and give it time. He explained that God has a way of working things out. He said that he hoped so because he has tried everything, but nothing seemed to work.

Every night before he contacts the local law enforcement to inform them that he is going home, he ponders over all the things that he is going through at the house. He shakes his head. Each night he comes home, he never knows what he is going to walk into. He's hoping that tonight will be a good night, which means that she will not start complaining as soon as he walks in the door.

After looking outside, Kyra doesn't see anything strange. She does notice the sheriff car patrolling by. She decides to go outside and stand on the front porch while she finishes drinking her tea. She leans on the banister and thinks, what a beautiful night. When she turns to go into the house, she notices that her shoes keep sticking to the porch. She doesn't see anything right then, but when she grabs the doorknob to go back in, she feels a lot of goop on her hand. "What in the world!" she says. She goes inside and washes her hands and finds the same substance on her shoes. "Who would do something like this?" she grunts. She hopes that it is just the prank of children and not the childish antics of an adult. She doesn't feel like it was enough to alarm the sheriff tonight, but she plans on talking to someone about it in the morning.

∿

It's time for Thomas to leave the tower. He locks down the main door that leads to the radio room and walks down a short corridor. At the end of the corridor is a door that leads to the outside balcony. From this balcony are fifteen steps, then another platform and finally, fifteen steps that lead to the ground.

All the way down, Thomas is thinking. When he is just about to the end of the steps, he slips and falls about four steps before landing on the ground. The fall catches him off guard, and he lands on his back. "Oh, man, I can't be out of commission. There isn't anyone to replace me, and I know Dottie is not going to be happy if she has to wait on me too," he thinks. He lays there in a puddle for a moment, thankful that he did not hit his head and praying that nothing is broken.

∿

Feeling some frequent nudging, Tammy begins to come around. She hears voices asking her if she is all right. She is doing her best to focus as she looks around. She sees Jake sitting on the ground talking to a fellow officer. "Are you okay?" another officer asks her.

"Yes, I think so but what happened?" she replies.

"That is what we are trying to find out. We kept calling the radio, but no one responded. After a half hour went by, we decided to come out and check on you. That's when a fellow officer saw Jake trying to get up off the ground. He was obviously struggling and when he first spoke, he was stuttering. So far, the only thing that he could tell us was that you two came back to check out the mayor's house because the dogs seemed different. They were quiet and that wasn't normal, so you both wanted to double check to make sure everything was okay. The next thing he knew was that someone had thrown something on him. It was so thick that he had trouble breathing. And he could feel himself collapsing. He wasn't sure what happened to you," the officer says.

Tammy agreed with what Jake said, but the officer also wanted to know how they ended up at the entrance of the driveway? The fence where the dogs are kept is a good fifteen feet away. Tammy wasn't sure but felt that maybe in the struggle of trying to breathe, they had walked farther than they had realized. Everything was so out of focus then; anything could have happened.

The officer explained that there had been some call-ins and that they were trying to get her and Jake to follow up on them. When they did not get an answer, that is when they decided to come out. But right now, they just wanted to get them to the hospital for a complete exam. Once they were deemed to be okay, they would discuss more later.

~

After a short rest, Thomas gets up. He brushes himself off and slightly limps to the car. He notices that the bottom of his shoes is quite muddy. Once he sits in the driver's seat, he removes his shoes to beat off some of the mud, but it doesn't come off easily. It is too gummy. He realizes that the mud is stuck to something sticky. Now he believes that is why he lost his footing. Someone has played a nasty joke on him, and he is not pleased. He plans on calling the morning guy to warn him before he attempts to go up the stairs. He needs to be careful, so he won't fall as well. And he will also let the sheriff know that there has been some foul play going on.

When Thomas got home, he finds it is all quiet. He's feeling much better and believes that a nice soak in the tub with some Epsom salt will make everything all right. After he wakes ups, if he is feeling okay, he will not call the doctor. He doesn't believe in going to the doctor unless he has to. But as he is going to the bathroom, he notices a shadow. He quickly turns to see what it is. It is his son standing, staring.

"What's the matter son? I didn't mean to wake you. I was trying to be as quiet as possible. I'm sorry if I did. Or were you up attending to Grammy?"

The son said, "No. I was up because I thought you were Mom. I heard her making some noise earlier and when I called out to her, she said to go away. She was fine. When I tried to go back to sleep, I heard some bumping sounds. I wanted to check on her again, but I didn't. That was about twenty minutes ago. I thought that you were her going into the bathroom."

As he stood listening, Thomas thought to himself that he hoped that his wife had not done the unmentionable in his home. He had warned her before about bringing something bad into the house. He could not control what she did on the outside, but he did not want his home tarnished. He just smiled and told his son that he was sure she was okay and to go back to bed.

The son hugged him and said, "I'm glad that you are home, Daddy. I like it when you are home."

"I like being home with you, too, son," Thomas replied. At the same time, both said I love you, and the son went back to bed.

"Now this, with all that I have been through tonight." Thomas shook his head as he thought. Then he said, "Well, let me check on Mom first to make sure she is all right. Then, I will take my bath and relax. I need to relax before I deal with that woman. I won't say anything tonight because I need some sleep. But tomorrow after TJ goes to school, I will get to the bottom of this."

He looks in on his mom, and she is resting well. She wakes a little and says "Tom, you're home? Had a good day?"

"Yes, Momma," he replied.

"Do you need anything, any help?"

"No, baby," she says.

"Okay," he says as he kisses her on the forehead. "See you in the morning."

He goes into the bathroom and draws his water. As he waits for the tub to fill, he rests his head in his hand and wonders. Then after thirty minute or so in the tub, he dries off and goes into the bedroom, but his wife is not there.

"That's it. Enough is enough!" he says.

～

Back at the station, the phones are steadily ringing. The officers have returned. "We left Tammy and Jake at the hospital. They seem to be fine. Jake's girlfriend and Tammy's mom have been notified and will take them home when they are ready," one of the officers said.

"Now what's going on?" he asked.

"Well, the mayor wanted to know what all of the commotion was about. Dr. Dan called back again to say that no one had shown up at his house yet. I told him that we were still trying the reach the officers out on patrol. Mrs. Phillips called and said something was spooking her cats. They have been hissing a lot while sitting on the window ledge. She thought she had heard something outside but was too afraid to go out to look. I told her that we will send someone out just as soon as we could. And Mr. Monroe, the barber, went back to his shop because he thought he had forgotten to set the alarm. When he returned, someone had thrown goop all over his bench out front. When he went back home, that same goop was on his front porch chairs. He wanted to know what was going on. He said he didn't see anyone, but they must have been watching him because his bench wasn't that way when he left. And his porch wasn't messed up when he first came home," said Dave, the night front-desk clerk.

"So what's the story with Tam and Jake?" Dave questioned.

Sergeant Bob, who is in charge said, "Mike, go find Wilson. I need you two to follow-up on these complaints. I want you two to stay together and phone immediately if anything seems suspicious. Start with Dr. Dan's house since he called first."

"All right," Mike replied. He went to the back to get Wilson. Wilson was called in tonight because it seemed as though it was going to be a busy night, and they did not know what had happened to Tammy and Jake. He had stayed in the building with Dave so he wouldn't be by himself. He still hadn't quite gotten the sleep out of his eyes. So Dave told him that he could rest in the back. He would call him if he needed him.

Mike came from the back and asked, "Where's Wilson?"

"Uh, I don't know. I thought he was lying down," Dave responded.

They all go to the back, but Wilson isn't there. Puzzled, Bob asked, "What in the world is going on around here?"

Then, suddenly, they heard a noise coming from outside. They rushed to the door, and when they opened it, there was Wilson. "Man, what are you doing?" Bob said with force.

"Uh, sorry, guys. I thought that the fresh air would help me gain my composure. So I stepped outside for a minute. My bad," he says.

"Man, I know we got you up to come in, but you need to let someone know when you step away like that. Anything could have happened to you, and no one would have known, "Mike said.

"Yeah, you are right. Sorry about that. Won't do that again," Wilson replied. Bob patted him on the back and said, "I need you to go with Mike to follow-up on some calls. Look, stay together, okay? And give us a call each time after you find out what the problem is."

"Got it," Wilson said. Then he and Mike left.

After Bob takes a deep breath and blows out a sigh of relief, he says to Julie, the other female officer on night duty, "I know there are equal rights here, but if you don't mind, can you make us a fresh pot of coffee? I need it."

"No problem," Julie replies.

He goes on to say, "Well, Dave, we found Jake stumbling around, somewhat confused. He had some sticky stuff on his face, but it wasn't that much. He was pulling at his skin like something was wrong. He kept saying, "I can't breathe, I can't breathe,"

Tam was lying on the curve somewhat hanging in the street. Julie went over to assist her. The most we could find out was that they were investigating the mayor's house and someone threw something on them. It caused them to lose focus. They didn't see who it was. And, of course, to make sure they were all right, we took them to the hospital. They will give us more information tomorrow after they have had a chance to get themselves together."

The phone rings again. "It's the mayor," Dave says. "Hello, Mayor, Sarge just got in. Hold on a minute."

"What do I tell him?"

"Just let him know that one of the officers was not feeling well, but everything is under control. And that's it. He doesn't need to know everything in full detail. We don't even know everything at this point. So let's satisfy him with an answer and then we will wait to see what Tam and Jake say tomorrow," Bob replies.

After Dave gets off the phone, about ten minutes later, the phone rings again. It's Mike, and he says that the Sarge needs to get over here. "I can tell it's going to be a long night," Bob says. So he and Richard left out immediately. That left Julie, Kevin, and Sam in the office with Dave.

～

"What do you think is going on, Sarge?" Richard asks.

"I'm not sure, and I'm almost afraid to find out. Have you ever woke having a feeling that something just wasn't right?" Bob asks.

"No, not really, Sarge. But you always say some weird things." Richard chuckles.

"Laugh as you will, but I'm telling you, there is more to life than what we can see. I sometimes feel as though someone is watching me, but for the life of me, I can't see of anybody. I once had a dream..."

But Richard stops him before he can finish and says, "Sarge, I don't mean to interrupt you, but your stories sometimes freak me out. There's too much crazy going on tonight. Can you save it for another time?"

They both laugh, and Bob says, "I got you. Yeah, you are right. This ain't the best time."

⌇

Back at the office, Mr. Monroe and Mrs. Phillips call again. "We are working on it," Dave says. "If it is not a problem, we may not be able to get to you until the morning. Will that be okay?" They both say that would be fine. Mrs. Phillips reminds Dave that she lives alone. Dave says that he knows and understands, then places her on hold. "Kevin, do you think that you could go out and calm Mrs. Phillips? She's really nervous."

Kevin says, "Sure. Julie and I will make a quick run to her house and come right back. It's probably that tom cat after her cats again." They all chuckle.

"Thanks," Dave says. He informs Mrs. Phillips that someone will be right out. She is grateful and says, "Thank you, thank you, thank you, sir"!

⌇

Before Bob and Richard reach the doctor's home, they see three young boys and a girl on the side of the road. They all have on backpacks and hiking boots. After a couple blast of the sirens, Bob pulls over. "What are you kids doing out this time of the night?" Richard recognizes a couple of them.

"George, Phillip, is that you?" Richard asks. They nod. "What are you all doing, and who are these two other kids with you?" At first, they are all silent. "Speak up, or we will take you back to the office. I'm sure you will have a lot to say then," Bob says.

"Not really," one of the children says, but neither Bob nor Richard saw who said it.

"What's that? Speak up! Someone got something to say. Say it. But you better be careful of how you say it or you will be in more trouble than what you are. Right now, we are concerned about you. But if you want to make this an issue, we can make it an issue," Richard says.

No one says anything, so Bob says, "All right, let's start again, "Why are you all out here?" Still no one says anything.

Richard walks to the girl, thinking that she will be easier to reason with. The entire time she has kept her head down. As Richard approaches her, he notices something. He sees she is not a girl. She is a young lad. "Look up," Richard says. He looks up. "What's your name? he asks.

"Mara," he says.

"Mara?" Richard questions.

"It was Marcus, but I want to be called Mara," he says.

"Why did you change your name" Richard asks? The lad looks at him frustrated and doesn't answer. "Okay" Richard said. "Can you tell me why you all are out here?" He answers but speaks so low that Richard can't understand what he is saying. "What?" Richard asks.

George yells, "We're leaving this place!"

Bob walks to him and asks, "You have a problem with us, son?"

"No," George says.

"Then why are you yelling?" he replies.

"I don't know," George whispers.

"Say it again, but this time, say it loud enough without yelling," Bob tells him.

"I don't know why I yelled, sir," he says.

"That's better. Now what and why are you all out here? This is the last time that we are going to ask you. If you don't answer this time, we are taking you all in," Bob says.

Then Mara answers and says, "It's because of me."

They all turn toward him as he speaks. "I've been abused by my father for a long time. He told me that I was abnormal and that he knew how to make me normal. So he would blacken my eye, bust my lip, or whatever. He broke my arm a few days ago, and I decided then that I had to leave. It was either I had to leave, or he would kill me. I thought about killing him, but I couldn't bring myself to do it. So I left. These are my friends. George is my special friend. Phillip and Tony are special friends. We heard about a place where people like us can live in peace, and we were trying to get there."

As he was talking, Bob and Richard looked at him closer and noticed that his left arm was in a sling. They also noticed the places on his face that looked as though they were old wounds.

"Sorry about that, son," Bob says.

Then George says, "Yeah, we left at night and were going through the woods so that no one would see us. We wanted to take the bus, but we thought we could reach the city in a few days by walking. We didn't have a lot of money, and we wanted to save it. But something strange happened that spooked us, and we came to the edge of the street. I wanted to investigate, but Mara didn't want me to. He was too afraid that I would get hurt, and he would lose me."

"Yeah," Mara replied. "I don't think I could go on if something happened to George."

"What spooked you?" Bob and Richard ask at the same time.

"A noise, no a vibration, no wait, a vibration that made a noise," George says.

"What's strange about that?" Richard asks.

"You would have to hear it," Mara responds.

All the kids shook their heads. Then Phillip says, "We could feel the vibration go all through our bodies. It made our stomachs feel funny. At first, it sounded like a hum but then it got louder, and the vibration started. Not real loud but loud enough to make us feel like we were going to come up on it."

Tony says, "And it sounded like we could hear whispers. That's when we decided to come to the highway."

"Yeah," George says. "It was like, someone was watching us, but we couldn't see them. And as we were trying to leave, Phillip..." George looks at the rest of the group and stops talking.

"Go on, and then what?" Bob asks.

George, again looks around at the other lads, and says, "We felt something."

"Felt something? Felt what?" Bob asks.

Hesitantly, George says, "Wet. We felt something wet."

Bob and Richard began to chuckle. "That was probably moisture from the tree leaves," Bob says.

"No, sir, no, sir. It wasn't," they insisted.

"Well, why not?" Richard asks.

"Because it was cold and gummy. Like hot glue, but cold, real cold," Mara says.

"Yeah. We yelled and ran. We were just peeling it off when you came up. See, I still have a little bit on me," Phillip says. He shows it to the officers, and they look at each other, puzzled.

"Hmm, that is a little strange," Richard says.

"I think it is just sap," Bob says, and he threw it to the ground. "But there's still the problem with you all being minors and on your own. We can't allow that."

Mara says, "I ain't going back to my dad!"

Both officers agree that the matter needs to be investigated. Mara asks if they can go to his aunt's house. This is his mother's sister. She was always kind to him and his friends. He is sure she won't mind them staying there until things could be worked out. She lives just a few blocks away.

The officers agree to take them there instead of letting them walk. Plus, they will have to contact an adult anyway. The lads get into the patrol car and goes to the aunt's home. It is very late, but she is not upset. She knows that her nephew is going through a lot, and the family is trying to resolve the issue without having to bring it out into the public. But now, she realizes that something must be done and done immediately. She promises to contact the lad's relatives in the morning and let them know what was going on. On her assurance, the officers agree to let the lads stay for the night. But she has to call in by noon to give an update on the situation. And someone will be out to talk with her.

~

Bob and Richard again head to the doctor's house. Bob phones in what happened to give a report and to let the doc know that they were still on their way. Then, Richard remembers something. "Hey, Sarge," he says.

"Yeah," he replies.

"The lads said something cold and sticky."

"Yeah, I know, crazy right," Bob replies.

Maybe, but Tam and Jake said something sticky was on them too," Richard says.

Then Bob stops the car and looks at Richard.

~

Finally, Bob and Richard reach the doctor's house. Before they could knock, Mike opens the door. "Thanks for coming out," he says.

"What's problem?" Bob asks.

"It's easier to show you than to tell you," the doctor replies. "Come on down to the basement. That's where I do my private work."

Bob and Richard look at each other because they didn't know that the doctor works out of his home as well as his office. The doctor notices the expression on their faces says, "Uh, yeah, I have some patients who don't want others to know that they have something going on." He nervously chuckles as he speaks. He goes on to say, "I try to accommodate my clients as much as I possibly can."

Bob looks at Mike and Wilson and tell them to go check out Mrs. Phillips house not knowing that Dave has already sent two officers. He thinks that he and Richard can handle whatever is going on here. "Don't forget to radio Dave and let him know that you two are moving on to the next call," Bob says.

"All right," they say as they leave.

After going down a flight of stairs, they reach a corridor that has a door at each end of the hallway. They turn to the right. Richard points to the left and asks, "Where does that door lead?"

"That's the way they come in," the doctor replies. "I use my side door for my professional business. Then I escort them into this door. In here is my office and examination room. It used to be my garage, but now I have a detached garage in the back."

The doctor opens the door to a huge chemical smelling room with a few nice chairs placed along the wall near a desk and file cabinets. There is a partition separating the sitting area from the work area. "It's behind here," the doctor says.

He pulls back the partitions and there are two examining tables and all types of medical equipment and supplies. Bob's and Richard's mouths drop because the carts and supplies are extremely disturbed. Things are thrown around like in a fit of rage.

"Did you make someone mad?" Bob asks.

"Not that I'm aware of," the doc replies. All I know is that I woke to loud sounds. I crept down here with a weapon, and halfway down, the noise stopped."

"Why didn't you call us before you started snooping?" Bob asks.

"I guess it was just my adrenaline rushing," he responds. I turned on the lights, and this is what I saw."

"Does it look like anything is missing?" Richard asks.

"Not that I can tell," the doctor replies. "But it's all very strange."

"What do you mean when you say all? "Bob asks.

"Well, the noise stopped immediately. No one came out. I didn't see any windows broken or opened. And the door that leads to the outside is hidden behind this partition here in the back. When I checked, it was still locked," the doctor responds.

"Come on, doc", Bob says.

"No, it's true," he replies.

"Maybe it locks behind you once you leave?" Richard says.

"Fellows, I don't mean to be disrespectful, but don't you think I know my own door?" the doctor replies. "The door has a deadbolt on it. You can't lock it without a key."

"Well, maybe someone has a key," Bob replies.

"Well, maybe. I plan on checking with my assistant later. She is the only one with a key, and I hope she nor one of her male friends didn't have anything to do with this. Plus, I think she gives most of her money to her boyfriend because he blows her phone up on paydays," the doc explains.

"That's probably it. But still it's a good thing you reported it. So we can deal with the situation more properly, and that will keep you out of trouble," Bob replies.

"But that ain't all, Sarge. Look at this," the doc says.

Bob and Richard take a closer look at the items. "I don't see anything," Bob says.

"Touch it," the doctor replies.

They touch different items. "It's sticky," Bob says as he looks at Richard, who is wide-eyed.

The doctor says, "Yes, and it's on the torn-up pieces of paper too."

"Can we have something for evidence?" Bob asks.

"Sure," the doctor replies. Then Bob goes on to say, "Yeah, we been having complaints about someone leaving sticky stuff all over town. What you've got going on over here may help us to narrow down who did it and what this stuff is."

"Yeah, that's what Mike and Wilson said. That's why they wanted you to see it for yourself. And while they were waiting for you, I tried to figure it out," the doctor replies. "It was really wet and gummy at first, but now it's just about dry. I've never seen anything like it before."

"Sorry about the wait. It's been a busy night," Bob says.

"That's okay. I truly understand. You know everything always seems to happen at once. Like the old saying goes, when it rains, it pours," the doc responses.

"You've got that right. And, tonight, its pouring," Richard says.

"Okay, fellows, I'm not going to hold you up any longer. Thanks for coming out," the doctor says.

"No problem,", they reply. "That's what we are here for," Bob says and Richards nods. Bob goes on to say, "But before we leave, let's just check all the house and the outside to make sure everything is okay. You got a lot of rooms here. Don't leave out anything. We want to make sure it is safe before we go."

After doing a thorough check, they get in the car. "What is going on?" Bob asks.

"I wish I knew," Richard responds.

"Well, I tell you what, whoever is responsible for this is going to be in a lot of trouble. They have assaulted our officers, damaged property, and who knows what else," Bob says.

Richard says, "Remember what the guys said? Remember, they heard something in the woods. Maybe we should go there to check it out."

"Maybe so. But not tonight. It's too dark right now. Let's try to get through all these situations right now and form a search party for tomorrow. You might be working some overtime. You up for that?" Bob responds.

"No problem, Sarge. My Helen understands what the job is like, so she doesn't give me any flack about it," Richard says.

"Yeah, she's a great lady," Bob replies.

"Yeah, I know. She keeps the kids in line and the house running smoothly when I'm not there. I couldn't have had a better wife if I asked for one," Richard adds.

"My Gladys is pretty special too," Bob says. "And you know what?"

"What, Sarge?" Richard asks.

"In times like these, you seem to appreciate them even more."

"You are so right, Sarge. You are most certainly right."

Bob radio back to the office to let Dave know they are okay but will fill them in with the details later. He does let him know that he thinks that they have a madman on the loose. Dave says that he is glad to hear from him and that he was wondering what was going on.

Bob said, "Yeah, I know we kind of took a long time. How is Mike and Wilson making out with Mrs. Phillips?" he asks.

"Mrs. Phillips?" "I sent Julie and Kevin to check on her."

"Julie and Kevin? "Did you tell Mike and Wilson that?" Bob questions.

"No, Sarge. I haven't heard from them since you left. I haven't heard from anybody," Dave responds.

"What?" Bob and Richard look at each other, stunned. "Look let me get back with you. "We are on our way to Mrs. Phillips' house. I will let you know when I get there," Bob replies.

"All right, Sarge," Dave replies. So down the road they fly.

⁓

On the way to Mrs. Phillips' house, Mike has to use the restroom. "What are doing, Mike?" Wilson asks.

"I'm pulling over. I have to go the restroom."

"Why didn't you do that while you were at the doc's?" Wilson asks?

"You know how it is, man. You have to go at the worst or the wrong time."

"Well, hurry up. "I'm still a little tired, and I want to get this night over. You already heard Sarge say that we may have to do overtime tomorrow, so we are only going to have a few hours of sleep before we have to come back to work," Wilson says.

"Yeah, yeah," Mike says as he gets out and goes among the trees.

While Mike is using the restroom, Wilson takes out some cannabis, lights and smokes it. "This is what I need to give me a little boost," he says to himself. He quickly takes a couple of puffs and puts it out. He gets out of the car and leaves the door open, hoping that the smell will dissipate, and Mike will not know the difference.

Mike comes back and says, "What are you doing?"

"Stretching my legs. You took so long that I started to come looking for you," Wilson says as he laughs.

"Come on, man, and stop clowning, Mike replies.

"See that's the problem tonight. Everybody is too stressed. I know this is serious stuff, but if we get too tensed up, it's going to wreck us. And what good will we be if we are all messed up? We have to stay as calm as possible. Yeah, not get to overheated so we can handle the situation properly," Wilson says.

"Not get too tensed up?" Mike questions.

"Yeah, relax."

"So you do this by taking a puff while you are working?" Mike responds.

Wilson turns and tries to answer, but he chokes up.

"Come on, man, what, do you think that I'm stupid or something. "I could smell that stuff where I was. I was hoping it was you because if it wasn't that meant someone was in the trees with me, and I didn't like the thought of that. There is enough strange stuff going on already. I had to believe it was you to keep from scaring myself out of my own shoes. Plus, you are giggling. Come on, man, you should know I know what's going on. I've been around the block a few times myself in the past. I ain't green, you know," Mike responds.

"Hey, you aren't going to tell Sarge, are you?" Wilson asks.

"Nah, man, this is just between us. But don't do that anymore while we are on our way somewhere. You don't want that smell on you when you go talk to people. Look in the glove compartment. I've got some air freshener in there. Spray yourself down when you get out. I know how it is. I'm not condemning you," Mike replies.

"Okay, and thanks," Wilson says.

"No problem," Mike responds.

Wilson looks in the glove compartment and says, "I don't see any spray."

"It's in there," Mike assures him.

"No, it's not," Wilson insists.

"It's in there. It's a small, thin, plastic bottle. See that's why you don't need to be doing what you just did. It makes you stupid. If you want to get stupid, get stupid on your own time, not the job's," Mike says.

He turns away slightly to try to find the bottle. Just as he does, they both see a really bright light, and Mike jerks the wheel sharply. They veer off into the woods and come to a stop when they hit a tree. The front of the car is smashed, and the airbags release. Smoke is coming from under the hood, and the two are struggling to get out. They don't want the car to ignite or explode while they are still inside.

~

Bob is frantic. He is wondering if his officers have been attacked like Tammy and Jake. He notices that to the east of him, the day is about to break, and he has not addressed all the citizens' concerns. He is trying to get to Mrs. Phillips' house as fast as he can. But not too fast because he's trying to see if something has happened to the officers along the way. Since no one has radioed, he fears the worst. He didn't say anything to Richard, but he could tell that they had the same thoughts as they looked at each other from time to time. Since the ride was extremely tense, they weren't as attentive as they thought that they were because they drove right past the faint beam of smoke coming from the trees.

They do see Mason's car pulled off to the side of the road. They stop to investigate and notice him sleeping. "Drunk again," Richard says.

"Yeah, we will deal with him on the way back," Bob says. They continue on to Mrs. Phillips' house.

~

Still, there was no sign of another patrol car. They decide to radio again to see if anyone called. They don't want to ask Mrs. Phillips because she may catch on that something is possibly wrong. She is already on edge.

When they radioed, Dave said that he had not talked to anyone, but it did seem as though someone was trying to contact the office. The radio had gone off, but when he tried to answer, he could only hear scuffling and some other strange noises. Bob and Richard knew that they had a situation on their hands. But, since they had already reached Mrs. Phillip's home, they decided to investigate that first. Bob instructed Dave to refer all concerns to the next shift. No one on the night shift could to leave unless it was an extreme emergency.

Before knocking on Mrs. Phillips' door, they take a walk around the premises. At first, everything seems to intact. Richard notices some more gummy stuff on the back doorknob and window seals. They go around to the front and knock. She doesn't answer. They try looking through the windows but can't see anything. They radio Dave again and ask him to call her to see if she will pick up. He does, but she still doesn't answer. So Bob decides to make a decision and bust in the door. He feels like that there is too much weird stuff going on and that they need to see if she is inside in distress.

After they kick the door in, they see her cats walking about, but Mrs. Phillips is nowhere to be found. A couple comes up to them crying as if they are trying to tell them something. Richard reaches down and picks up one and says, "I wish that you could tell me what is going on."

Before Bob calls in his report, they decide to check the garage. He thinks that if she was spooked, then maybe she went to a relative's home. But when they look inside, her car is still there. Bob radios in and tells Dave to put out a missing report for Mrs. Phillips due to her age. Dave tells the Sarge that Tammy has phoned in and said that she is all right. But he has not heard from Jake. Bob tells

Dave to call Tammy back and explain the situation with Mrs. Phillips. He doesn't want her to come in the office the next day. He wants her to stay at Mrs. Phillips' house just in case she shows up. If she returns to the house, he needs someone there to explain why the door was broken into and someone to look after her cats. He then tells Dave that they are on their way back to the office.

On the way back, Mason is still in the car. Richard asks Bob if he was going to stop. Bob says due the circumstances of everything going on that night, he would give Mason a break. He will talk to him later. He says that he wasn't too upset with him because at least he had enough sense to pull over and not drive in that condition. They don't stop and head back to the office.

~

Mason starts to come to and sees the patrol car going by. "Oh, no, it is just about daybreak." "My wife is going to have a hissy fit. Well, at least I didn't get arrested, and I don't see where they left a ticket on my car. So that's a good thing."

As he is trying to compose himself, he sees something strange when he looks in the rearview mirror. His face is wet and peeling. "What in the world?" he says.

Then he notices another set of lights coming directly toward him, like the car is driving down the wrong side of the road. They come up so fast that he does not have time to get himself together. And the lights are so bright that he cannot see anything. "What is the need for all of this," he says. He sees two walking toward him, one on each side of the vehicle.

∼

About the same time that Mason comes to, Mike and Wilson reach the main road, hoping that someone will come along and help them. They know that there is not usually that much traffic at this time of the morning, but they are still hopeful. Mike's radio is missing, but Wilson's is still by his side. He tries to call, but no one answers, so he thinks that it is broken.

As they look down the street, they see Mason's car and the bright lights. They are happy that someone is on the road. They begin to yell for help. As they do, a smaller light comes toward them. It reaches them so fast that they do not even hear the vehicle as it approaches. A tall shadow comes toward them. They say, "Help us, please. We need to get to the sheriff's office to let them know what has happened. From there we can call for an ambulance."

∼

Bob and Richard arrive back at the office, and they rush inside. As Bob hurries, he says, "Hey, did you hear anything from Mike and Wilson or Julie and Kevin?" To their astonishment, no one is there. "What in the world?" he says. Richard, stunned, stands there frozen.

"Dave, Dave," Bob yells. He looks at Richard and says, "Snap out of it, man. I don't need you to freak out on me as well." But Richard continues to stand there, not moving. Then Richard starts to stutter and point. Bob notices that Richard is not staring at the empty room, but he has turned around and is staring back at the door. He slowly turns around to see what has frightened him. He is afraid that Dave and the others have been killed and that they are lying on the floor. He is thinking that they just overlooked them in their haste to come in.

When he turns and looks toward the door, he sees deep scratches and wet handprints along the frame and wall. He starts to look around at the rest of the room. He sees splatter of wet, gummy substances all about. He looks back at Richard, who is horrified. Tears are running down his face, and he looks as though he trying to keep from screaming. Richard's eyes motions toward the door again. Bob doesn't say anything, but he is thinking, "Now what?" He slowly looks back at the door, and there is a bright light coming from the hallway. From that light, a tall figure steps forward.

～

For a moment, Thomas was sleeping well until a thump wakes him. "I guess that's the misses," he says. He lays there with his eyes closed, pretending to be asleep. He is not sure if he is going to say anything to her. He slightly opens one eye and looks at the clock. "Hmm, 5:00, how disgraceful," he thinks. "So she decides to come in just before daybreak."

A few more sounds are heard, but she still doesn't enter. After a couple of minutes, Thomas decides to confront her. When he leaves his bedroom, he notices his son's door is open. He peeks inside and sees that he is not in his bed.

"TJ", he gently calls, trying not to wake his mother. But he doesn't answer. He walks around looking for him and sees him looking out the front door. "TJ, what are you doing son?" he says. But still TJ doesn't respond. Very puzzled, again he speaks out to his son, "TJ, what's the matter with you? "Why aren't you answering me. Come away from that door," he insists.

TJ turns around and says, "I think that you will want to see this, Dad."

Thomas' face is no longer suspicious; it is frightened. TJ's face is covered with goo. As Thomas walks to him to find out what happened and why is he acting so strangely, he remembered the substance that was on the stairs at the station. "But who would do that to his son?" he asked himself. "And why is he just standing there, not doing anything?" Thomas goes to look out the front door and there he sees what has captured his son's attention.

∾

Kyra is awakened again. "Man, I am really having a problem sleeping tonight. And what is that bright light coming through my window?" she questions. She gets up to look outside, but she can't see too well. She can see people moving around but can't make out what's going on. It is still supposed to be a little dark outside, but there is glare that is obscuring her vision. She puts on her robe and goes outside to see what all the commotion is about.

She opens her door, and there on her porch is an extremely tall figure. She gasps when she sees it. She tries to turn and run, but the figure spews a wet, gooey substance onto her. She is partially frozen. She can hear, but she can't talk.

The figure looks her over as though it was not just looking at her outside but evaluating her thoughts. While it is staring at her, she is staring at it. It has enormously long, skinny arms with what seems to be two elbows. It raises its arm up to touch her on her chest. Her heart begins to palpitate much faster, and she can feel it pulling energy from her. She can see where the first elbow is causing its arm to turn as it touches her.

She looks down at its legs, and they have two knees. She looks to the side of her to watch them walk. They were approaching almost every door in the neighborhood, house and every establishment except the church. They stroll up and down the streets searching. As they walk, the extra joints allowed them to bend into various shapes so that they can easily reach around items. And their necks look like an accordion, which allowed them to stretch almost as long as their entire body.

Their heads are huge, just like the drawings of aliens she had seen before but never believed existed. But their faces almost look human, except for their skin. It glows and is dewy.

Then she thinks to herself that the one in front of her looks Native American. And as she looks around, the others resembled different races. She could see features that resembled Asians, Hispanics, Africans, Australians, Europeans, and so forth. When she looks back at the one in front of her, she even saw a similarity of her own family in it. "How could this be?" she thought. "Was it taking on my looks as it was examining me?"

Suddenly, it drops its arm, and the rest of them stop moving. They have everyone's attention, but strangely, there wasn't an animal in site, not even a bird. As she looks into the eyes of the one in front of her, it was smiling as though it can read her thoughts. Then, they all begin to speak. And this is what they said:

~

We have been here since the beginning of your time, and we watched you from the shadows. We knew that you were a weak specimen when you allowed one of the tree dwellers to beguile you. We sat back and watched as you turned on each other and killed your own flesh. We hoped that we could make a deal with you. A deal that would allow us to live as one and be great all over the land, a deal that would allow us to totally come out of the shadows.

So, we showed ourselves to you, and you were not afraid. You liked our power and desired it the same way you desired it from the tree dweller. But the tree dweller could only show you a way to obtain it. We possessed it, and you wanted it. We wanted your beauty, so we agreed to blend our bloods together.

As we blended, our features became more like yours. You bore us children, who grew great and became mighty warriors of the land. But, still, your ways were ununified. Great turmoil came across the land. Many of us and all but a few of you were put to sleep. And the ones of us who remained went back into the shadows.

After a while, from the land you rearose. This time you were more peaceful. And, again, we desired to share our power and knowledge with you so we could live outside of the shadows. When we came to you, you agreed and together we lived as one across the land.

We dwelled in caves together, and you drew pictures of us on the walls to memorialize our friendship. And, again, our offspring bore a great league of people. We built monuments to honor our blood born kings and queens. Our warriors were fierce and conquered all those who would not blend their blood with ours. We built waterways so that our bloodline would never hunger or thirst. From the shadows, we gave you special gifts. Gifts that your descendants have discovered, but still, unto this day, have not understood its mysteries or its power.

Then trouble came to some of us who lived in the rocks. So, we opened a portal that allowed you to walk among the shadows. The same way we were able to come into the light. And when the land became too volatile to stay, instead of waring, together we went into the portal, never to return.

But as time went on, many of you began to detest us. A New Blood came along. This blood was from the One who brought you forth from the dirt. You blended your blood with that blood. And our heritage began to die. Then you walked around casting us out. To keep from being destroyed, many of us returned to the shadows. But we knew that you would not remain faithful to the New Blood, either. Therefore, we waited.

As time went on, we saw you slipping away just as we thought you would. And we said that maybe you would desire us again. We waited for you to call out to us in our secret language. But you never did. Therefore, we decided to appear to you, but you were not the same. You were frightened. You had forgotten how we once lived in harmony. In anger, we took a few of you to the shadows.

There, we examined you to see why you were so different. We know that you knew about us because our drawings remain on the walls of the rocks. But, still, you were afraid. And when we let you return, you told horrible stories about what we have done. You made moving pictures of us displaying us as violent creatures, something that was only interested in destroying your kind. None of this was true. We only wanted to live in the light because the One who formed you from the dirt casted us into the shadows. But now we realized that by blending our blood with your blood, we created something vile. And we now know that we have no use for you.

We became angry and wanted revenge. This time, we went before the One who brought you from the dirt and that casted us into the shadows. We asked if we could have you to do with you as we pleased. The One said that we could have all who turned their backs on the New Blood. The One said that there was a great day coming. In that day, the New Blood would reward those faithful to the New Blood. The One told us that in that day, we would no longer be able to walk among the light. And, before we go into the shadows, we are to take you with us. We have taken some of you already. Because this land is now being transformed, whereas only the New Blood, the One who brought you from the dirt and its faithful, will dwell in it forever. Here, there will be no more birthing and no more dying, no more blending of bloods.

~

As they spoke, Kyra eyes continued to look around. As far as she could see to the west, it was light. She knows that the figures are causing it because it isn't quite daybreak, and the west is always darker than where she is.

She knows what they mean when they said New Blood. Tears begin to roll down her face. But not for fear this time. She wished that she had listened to the ones who told her that there was something greater than her. But she didn't believe in anything that she could not physically see or touch. She now realizes that the signs were there all the time, but she chose to ignore them. And now she realizes that she did feel the touch, but it was in her heart. Before she thought that it was only the craftiness of her own mind and ability that gave her those feelings and ideas. Now she has to admit that she was wrong. And as she looks at her neighbors, many of them are realizing the same thing.

All the things that irritated her about other people didn't matter anymore. All the people whom she turned her back on, she looked within herself, saw their faces, and wept even harder. Oh, how she wished that she had been kinder. She wished that she could have another day to make a difference in a better way. Unfortunately, it was too late to turn back. It was too late for all of those who ignored the new blood and didn't remain faithful. She said within herself that the figures may have come from the shadows, but we were the ones in the dark.

Then a rumbling vibration brought her back to the consciousness of what was taking place. And a loud sound pierced the atmosphere along with sounds of explosions. To the northeast of her, she could see great flames of fire and smoke bursting through the air. Once the rumbling vibrations began, all the figures stopped talking. Their ears moved around as though they were waiting for a signal. Suddenly, they opened their mouths wide and goo spewed out over all the people. And with an enormous flash of light, it was over.

Bonus Reads

The Gift and The Trip

THE GİFT

Introduction: The Gift

From her youth to a young woman, a girl desperately desires to be fulfilled. Many deep hurts prevent her from fully trusting people. But one day, she gets a gift, one that frees her heart and clears her troubled mind. From that moment on, nothing will ever be the same.

TRUE LOVE NEVER DiES

E veryone has a gift. Sometimes certain things must happen before we realize what our gift is. I remember when I found out what my gift was. But I did not find out suddenly. It began to manifest itself to me in the winter of 1973. I was about eight years old and attending my mother's funeral. This was absolutely the saddest day of my life. I could not stop staring at the coffin and the big hole that lay beneath her final resting bed. I could see a man speaking, but I could not hear what he was saying. I could see everyone crying, but I could not hear them sobbing. The whole scene seemed like a silent movie playing before my eyes.

To ease the pain, I began to reflect back to a short time before my mother died. I was visiting her at the hospital. She was lying in the bed with her eyes open but looking up and staring at something in a distance, rarely glancing at anyone. Several people, mostly relatives, were there whimpering. I began to sing and dance, hoping that I would get my mother's attention. Even though she would look my way, for some reason I felt that she did not see me. Yet I was not sure. I was holding on to the thought that if she could not see me, maybe she could hear me. I hoped that she would not die if she knew I was still waiting for her to get better. I just knew that she loved me and I wanted her to know now more than ever that I loved her. She once told me that true love never dies. So I just could not stop loving her. I had to give her a reason to hold on until she could heal and come home. So I sang and danced, and I tried to smile as I fought back the tears waiting to burst from my eyes.

My display seemed to upset most of the people there. They told me to be quiet because I would disturb the other patients. Reluctantly, I stopped. I slowly glanced at each person in the room as the tears ran down my face. I thought to myself, *Do they not know that if I stop showing her I love her, she might give up?* I felt that they did not love her as much as I did. And I knew that they did not need her like I did. All of their faces were in disgust toward me except for an aunt and a man whom I had often seen before. The two of them smiled as tears ran down their faces.

I heard one of my relatives say in regard to my crying that I was just upset because my mother was dying. This was partially true. I was more upset because many of my relatives never valued how I felt. I was always discouraged when I shared my opinions. Therefore, I learned to keep my feelings to myself, except for occasionally talking to my imaginary playmates. And yes, of course, I was upset because my mother was dying. *Who wouldn't be?* I mumbled.

If my mother was to die, it was already discussed that my aunt who was smiling would become my primary caregiver. I was not sure who the man was. I had seen him around town, but we had never been introduced. He had a calm aura about him. My mother must have liked him a lot because he visited the hospital quite a bit. She often stared at him more than the rest of us. He could have been one of her male friends. I know she used to keep male company, but she never introduced them to me. One day I asked her why she did not introduce them. She said that if one of them were to become my daddy, she would. Since she never remarried, I never met any of them directly. However, there were two other men who used to do a lot of nice things for her and who went out of their way to speak to her as she passed through the streets. So I kind of thought they were or at least wanted to be her friend. Anyway, none of that was important to me anymore. I did not want a daddy. I wanted my mother to live.

As I focused back to the memorial service, I noticed that the man at the hospital and the two men who went out of their way to get my mother's attention were there as well. *Real good friends they must be*, I thought to myself. *There to the very end.*

That is what I most desired, good friends, people I could share everything with, laugh with, trust in, and gently tell me when I was wrong. Most importantly, they had to like me just because of who I am. In return, I would be just as good of a friend to them.

A squeaky noise brought me back to the casket and the hole beneath it. It was the noise of the crank lowering the coffin in the ground. This was devastating to me. All of a sudden, my silent picture was filled with the noise of my own voice screaming. No! I pleaded. *Please do not lower her! She is not dead! I just know it! If you just give her some more time, she will get up!* I bolted toward the casket in attempts to stop the man from turning the crank, but my aunt caught me and held me in place. I could not focus any longer. I folded and fell to the ground.

I do not remember what happened after that. I just remember lying in my bed with my back toward the door, staring at the wall. My mother and I used to share the same room. Back then the room always felt warm in the frosty winter nights. Not anymore, especially that night. That night seemed abnormally cold, almost like the freezer at a meat-packing company my class once visited.

To help me warm up, I wrapped the covers around me twice. There was no one in the room with me to talk to. Even my imaginary friends left me that night. I just lay there and listened to the quietness. I could not seem to sleep. At a distance I heard someone walking downstairs toward the staircase. The floors were hardwood covered with linoleum rugs that crackled whenever someone walked on them. Usually I could recognize everyone's footsteps. These I did not.

Slowly the footsteps crept up the staircase. Once at the top, they came toward my room, which was in the back of the house. I had always had a vivid imagination, and therefore I thought the worst. So when the footsteps reached the doorway of my room, I was literally shaking. I just knew that someone was there to kill me. I almost welcomed the thought.

While my mother was in the hospital, I would hear other people sit around and tell death stories. I hated that! It was like my mother had already died. They did not give her any hope to live. To hear this was especially hard for me. Before my mother got ill, death never entered my mind. Now it seemed as though death was all I thought about. On one of those occasions, I wanted to be the one who was dying instead of her. Everyone liked her, and no one seemed to like me.

While in the bed, I felt a constant flow of cold air blowing on the back of my head. It was like someone was standing close behind me breathing slowly, steady and deep. I called out to see if anyone would answer, but no one did. My mother always taught me to pray before I went to sleep, so this was the only thing I could think to do. I began to pray though I did not believe that praying would make a difference. Most of my prayers seemed like wasteful babblings. I prayed that my mother would not leave me, but she did.

When I prayed, I requested to fall asleep so I would not know when I was killed. Since I wondered what death was like, I also asked if being dead was like being in a long, deep sleep. If the answer was yes, then I wanted to just wake up in the morning, not remembering when I fell asleep. If the answer was no, then this meant I would die. If I was to die then I did not want to feel the person killing me.

The answer must have been yes, because I woke up. I opened my eyes to a brightly lit sky. I could hear my family outside of my room wondering how long I was going to be asleep. I smiled and thanked God for answering my prayers this time. So from that point on, I believe that death is like being in a deep sleep. I forgot to ask what you dream about. So what happens after that, I am not sure. I then began to wonder if I was dreaming when I heard the footsteps and felt the cold air. Again, I really did not care. The first night of knowing that my mother was not coming back was hard enough. I just wanted to move on. I had bigger fish to fry. How to live without her was the only thing on my mind.

Everyone has Problems

———— ⁓ ————

About eight years later my aunt asked me if I remembered the day I tried to console my mother by dancing and singing. *Of course*, I replied. She then told me what I felt all along. She said that she knew my mother could hear me and that she was pleased. She also said that she knew her sister better than anyone else and that she knew what made her happy. She believed that the singing and dancing truly did. When she said that, it was one of the few moments in my life when I felt that someone appreciated me for who I was.

As for the man, I would see him around from time to time. He was some type of missionary, because he visited often when someone was sick. Each time I tried to approach him; he seemed to be in a hurry to leave. I once managed to say hello. He looked at me, nodded his head, and smiled. Before I could muster up more of a conversation, someone distracted my attention. *Oh well, I thought, I'll just leave him alone and let him do his work. At least he is doing a good deed.*

There were several missionary people around town. They must have been from a missionary church, school, or something. I was not that fond of churches even though I attended one. They preached a lot of things, but I did not see where they had a great impact or change for the better. There had been times when great church leaders had been caught doing the very thing they condemned others for. My aunt said that people are the same everywhere, in and out of church, and we all have some type of problem. She believes that the difference with church people and people who do not go to church is that church people have admitted that they have problems. They go to church in belief that God will heal all their problems. She said I should not be too hard on people. I did agree with her. It was just that I felt that if church people knew that they made the same mistakes as non-church people, then they should not point their fingers at others as much as they did.

I believe that is why I liked the missionaries. I could really see what they were doing. They did not just console people in the hospitals and at funerals. They worked along with people in the church. They walked along beside people as they crossed the street, helped people lift heavy items, and so on. I even saw a missionary ride to the airport and walk with the person to the plane. I supposed the person was nervous about flying, so the missionary went along to comfort him. I wished everyone would have a helping spirit. But unfortunately, everyone does not.

For instance, a couple of years ago, I saw two men fighting in the park. The motion of their scuffing is what captured my attention. I could not stop staring as they threw blows and wrestled with each other. Several people were watching as well but most of the people were trying to stay out of the way in fear of getting hurt.

Three men were so close to the two fighting that they could touch them. Since they were that close, I thought they were all together. Two of them were encouraging one of the men fighting by waving their fists, and shouting like a couple of cheerleaders at a pep rally. The third man just stared as though he was watching the Sunday night matinee.

A lady, watching from a distance, ran screaming for the police. When one of the two men boosting the fight heard the lady yelling, he pulled a knife out of his pocket. He then threw it to his friend who had his opponent held face down. Both men seemed exhausted, but the one on the ground seemed more injured. The man who threw the knife yelled, "Finish it, the police are coming." With one hard thrust, the knife was slammed into the opponent's back. People began to scream as they tried to get clear of the violence. The two men rooting and the one with the knife ran away. I later saw on the news that the three of them were caught. The news did not say anything about the man watching. I often wondered if the man watching snitched on his friends. If he did, he did a heroic act. Many people will keep quiet in fear of being killed themselves. But there is a part of me that hoped that he did squeal. Maybe it is because I did not like the way he just stood there and watched. Yet, I could tell that he did not feel like the other two men. He did not seem pleased at all.

However he did nothing to stop the fight or to talk his friend out of throwing the knife. But I supposed he was just like most of us, more concerned with self-preservation. I believe that everyone has someone or something in his or her life that he or she is afraid to stand up to in fear of what might happen. I can truly say that fear of what others would do or say has always been a struggle for me.

THE REVIVAL

B y the time I was twenty-one years old, I worked
full-time in the city hospital as a caregiver. I
chose to work there because it was the place
where most people went if they did not have insurance,
and I like to help needy people. Plus, it was the place
where my mother died. I chose to be a caregiver because
I always wished that I could have done more for my
mother. Since I was so little then, I was not able to help
her like I wanted to. So, I promised myself that when I
got older, I would help as many people as possible. At
the moment, I did not see myself as much of a help. But
I knew that one encounter can make all the difference
in the world.

I usually arrived at work about 6:00 a.m. After checking
each patient's charts to read what the previous caretakers
wrote, I began to make my routine bed checks. That
morning, I was moving a little slower than normal, still a
little tired from my previous night's venture. About 5:00
p.m., I went walking because there was a lot on my mind.
I reflected back on many things. One thing that bothered
me was one of the missionaries.

Just a few days ago, my aunt and I were visiting a sick friend's house when the daughter came out screaming and crying. "He's gone! I do not know what I will do now that he is gone." As we escorted her back inside, my aunt tried to console her. My aunt asked me to phone the coroner. There was a missionary standing beside the bed. I looked over at him and asked him if he had called the police or anyone else. He shook his head. That frustrated me a little. I thought that it was nice to visit, but not to just stand there when things like this happened. Offer some help to the family. Instead he smiled and nodded, as they often do, before he walked off. *Well*, I grunted. *Now he was acting much like the other church people. They preach a lot of things, but their follow-through leaves little to be admired.*

As I continued to walk, I also wondered about my work at the hospital. There was still a lingering feeling of being unfulfilled. I did not know how to fill that void. In a couple of more days, it would be my friend's father's funeral. I was not ready for that either. The occurrence with the missionary left me in no mood for hearing a sermon. I did not want to hear another lecture on how we should be there for each other in times of need. And when that time comes, no one is there but one or two people who truly love you.

Not to my surprise, what was it that I could hear from a distance but a church revival taking place in the local park? The foot stomping and hand clapping could not be contained by the canvas walls. *Wow*, I said. *What irony.*

The very thing that I was not in a mood for was the very thing I stumbled upon.

There is one thing that I did learn about God. And that is that He will make you face what you want to avoid. Any other time I would have just walked in a different direction. For some reason, I drew closer and closer until I found myself being ushered to a seat. The music was very upbeat. It was strange how I felt that this was what I needed to clear my head even though I tried to fight the feeling.

As good as the music was, I promised myself that I would leave soon because it was getting late. I had to get up by 4:30 a.m. in order to get to work on time; plus, I did not want to hear the message. Yet each time I thought about leaving, I was too embarrassed to walk past an usher who seemed to stare my way and detect my nervousness. We frequently connected eye to eye. So I kept saying to myself, *I will leave in five more minutes.* Five minutes turned into ten and so on. Soon, I began to stop watching my watch and let the ambiance take me over.

The congregation jumped, shouted, and praised as their hearts were touched. More and more, I was becoming enslaved to the commotion. It soothed and invigorated me. It gently swept me off my feet and held me like a mother cradling her child. As the spirit flowed from front to back, and chair to chair, I could no longer contain myself. I too shared in the moment. Tears ran down my face.

When the speaker came to the podium, the music slowly softened. By this time in my life, I had fully stopped going to church. But I remembered that the music softening was the way people knew to let their emotions calm down and to prepare for the message. The speaker came out singing, and before you knew it, the commotion rekindled like fresh logs added to a quieting fire. This time I could not hold back. I sang and clapped my hands. Just doing that gave me a calm sense of relief.

Eventually the speaker began his message. There was something different about him. I was not quite sure what it was. Maybe it was the way his deep voice echoed in my ear. It was not just me. Everyone's eyes locked on him as though we were in a trance. We nodded up and down, shouted, and wiped tears from our eyes. I thought to myself how emotionally satisfying his message was. Especially when he said, "Everyone has a purpose in life. Everyone has a gift. A gift is just what it is, a gift. It is something you have that should be given to someone else because it is something someone else needs. That is why it is not for you to keep to yourself. The gift is already inside you. Since it is inside you, you always have it to enjoy. Others do not have what you have, but they need what you have. Not only do they need your gift, they will enjoy it. What is your gift you ask? Ask God! For the Bible says every good and perfect gift comes from above. God assigned it to you; therefore, God can show you what it is. Let God guide you on how to use your gift. As you use it, others will benefit and you will be blessed. It may not always be easy, but you will always be satisfied. Once satisfied, you will become happy. In turn, you and your purpose will be fulfilled."

Those words riveted through my head all night. I wondered what my gift was. So quietly before I fell to sleep, I mumbled a few words to God. *God, I have not talked to You in a very long time. Yes, my mother wanted me to trust in You. I tried, but my disappointments seemed to be more prevalent than You. So if You do not want to be bothered with me, I truly understand. I heard tonight so many things. The speaker said that You do not look on the outside but on the heart of man. You know what is needed in order to be satisfied. One way to be satisfied is to use our gift. Show me my gift so that I can be satisfied. Guide me so that I can be blessed.* As I fell to sleep, I wondered if God even cared enough to answer me. *Why should He?* I thought. *No one else seems to.* At that time, I had no idea what my prayer was about to unfold.

Filled with Amazement

T ired or not, I had to shake myself and focus. I was at work. These people depend on me. What many take for granted, others would give all they have to regain—their health. My mind wandered again and questioned if giving care was my gift. I did provide comfort and care to the critically ill and dying. *Hmm*, I thought. *Maybe my voice will be the last voice they hear. Wow, this must be my gift! Yes, this must be it. I have to be comforting each time I see them. No, it is not a pleasant job, but they need me.* While deeply reflecting inside, my heart began to pound harder and harder. It was jumping with joy. *God did answer me!*, I silently mumbled. *Therefore, He must care because He answered me!*

Filled with amazement, I stared down the hallway. The floor twinkled like a crystal lake shimmering under a glistening moonlit night. There were six rooms to each hallway and four hallways to each wing. I worked on the annex wing along with a head nurse, a couple of floor nurses, and three other attendants like myself. Each attendant is responsible for one hallway. On my hallway, I had six patients: Mrs. Tanner, Ms. Conner,

Michael Winborne, Michele Doven, Kelley Pierce, and Mr. Riggers.

My first stop is always Mrs. Tanner, an eighty-six-year-old terminally ill mother of 9. She has a lot of things wrong with her. She is so skeletal that she looks like someone has literally sucked the juice right out of her. Her breathing is so shallow that I am surprised she is still here each time I arrive at work. She just stares off in the distance like my mother used to do. I talk to her a little bit, but she never responds. The only time she makes a noise is when I have to turn her. And then it is only a groan.

Usually I fly through her care because she does not speak. All of my other patients talk, so I spend more time in their rooms. But after hearing the sermon and believing that God answered my prayer, I had a change of heart. I thought back to when my mother was dying. Mrs. Tanner may be like her. My aunt said that my mother could hear me, and maybe she can too. More than ever, I was determined to give comfort and love to those who are dying, just like I wanted to do for my mother. It just might be that my love and concern will give my patients the desire to press on and live. Yes, I said. *This has to be my gift*.

So that day, I began my work differently. I was going to give Mrs. Tanner a nice, slow, comforting massage with her bath. She might or might not be able to respond to me. She might or might not live. These things really do not matter. Everyone needs to feel as though he or she is loved, especially in the end. So many times people give up on you when they think that you are dying. Unless it was someone close to me, I must admit that I too have been guilty of giving up. Not anymore was I going to feel that way. I planned to be what I had wanted others to be all of my life—there for me all the way to the end.

Code Blue

~~~

As I began to move toward Mrs. Tanner's room, one of the missionaries got off the elevator and headed to her room as well. I approached her to let her know that I would be bathing Mrs. Tanner and she would have to wait outside or come back later. *Excuse me,* I politely announced. Before I could finish my statement, a code blue went off in Mr. Rigger's room. *Please clear the hallway,* I told the missionary. *You can either sit in Mrs. Tanner's room until I return or wait downstairs. All patients' doors must be closed at this time.* She entered Mrs. Tanner's room.

This could be the day Mr. Rigger leaves us. His family had been visiting more frequently, sometimes spending the night. Mr. Rigger was a forty-seven-year-old war veteran. Before entering the military, he was a light smoker and a social drinker. After going into the service, he became a chain smoker and an alcoholic. Now he has cancer of the larynx. This was his sixth visit to my ward. His cancer had been in remission for two years from his last admission. Each visit he looked frailer and frailer. With this last visit, his skin was so pale that it turned gray.

The cancer seemed to be like a blood parasite, eating him from the inside out.

As the code alarm rang, one of his family members ran out of his room hysterically looking for help. I hurried to do my part. Other staff rushed to his aid. As I entered the room, the head nurse insisted that all other visitors had to leave. I noticed that there was a missionary who was leaning directly over Mr. Rigger. *Excuse me*, with a firm but polite voice I said to him. *You must leave now! You must stop leaning over him like that!* Some of the medical staff looked at me strangely. Maybe I was too rough. Maybe it was not my place to give the command.

As the missionary left, the head nurse asked me to go out and console the family while they worked diligently on Mr. Rigger. When I left the room, I noticed that the missionary who was in Mr. Rigger's room stopped to talk with the missionary in Mrs. Tanner's room. The two whispered, shook hands, and the one from Mrs. Tanner's room patted the other on his back, like she was congratulating him. This made me think back to when my friend's father died. The missionary did nothing to help. Now a missionary was standing over Mr. Rigger and another one pats him on his back. I wondered what their true purpose was. Were they here to help or harm? Did they have some type of secret mission to rid the world of the weak and feeble? I found myself standing still, trembling with fear as all the thoughts ran through my head.

Before I could make it to where the family was gathered, the intern walked out of the room, passed me, and said,

"Hopefully he is in a better place now." A sick feeling came to my stomach. I was sad for the family, but I feared that there was something more sinister going on. For now, I would just go on and attend to the rest of my patients. But I would keep a watchful eye for anything else that might occur.

THE BICYCLERS

O nce back at the nurse's station, I discussed my thoughts with another caregiver. She laughed and thought I was under too much stress. As I went on, I began to give her "the willies". I asked her if she had noticed anything suspicious. She said she had not. I also asked her what she thought about the missionaries. She thought that I was talking about the candy stripers. No, I told her, *the ones who come from the churches or some type of organization. They visit all of the time, not only here, but everywhere, supposing to help people.* She said she could not tell one church person from the other. She said she usually avoided them because she did not want to hear what they had to say. I tried to convince her that some of them were strange and possibly up to no good. They even looked very mysterious. It is something about the way they stared, rarely saying much, just walked and stared. As I listened to myself, I too thought I was a little cuckoo.

Wow, it has been a long day, I told my coworker. Instead of taking the subway straight home, I decided to go downtown to window shop and get something to eat.

She offered me a lift. *That would be great,* I said. *Then I could have a nice stroll home after I eat since so much had happened at work today.* I believed window shopping and a quiet dinner would help me relax.

My coworker dropped me off in front of my favorite shoe store. I love to shop for shoes. As I glanced through the window, I saw the reflection of two young men speeding and swerving through traffic on their ten- speed bikes. They were riding very recklessly, disregarding traffic signals and the basic rules of the road. In my opinion, many young people ride their bikes, their skateboards and walk as though the world only belongs to them. Unfortunately, these two were no exception.

As I looked closer, I noticed that one of the bicyclists looked a little different. I turned around to get a better glance. It was one of the missionaries. This made me chuckle because I wondered how he was providing service to the youth. He definitely was not helping him abide by the rules of the road. But then again, I guess they cannot be doing missionary work all of the time. Maybe they were just two friends hanging out. I chuckled again because this was truly an example of how people are often different when they are not doing their jobs. Any other time, the missionaries are calm, almost nonexistent. Now here was one of them speeding through the streets. Wow! But on the serious side, I also felt that if the two of them did not watch what they were doing, instead of leaving a streak through the air, they both would be a streak on the street. I just shook my head and continued to chuckle as I turned away.

Suddenly a couple of loud screeching sounds pierced the air, followed by a crashing noise with people yelling and running. I followed the crowd to see what happened. One of the young men on the bike had been hit by a van. The missionary was leaning over the young man, shaking his head. As I looked at them, the missionary turned and stared at me. I did not know why, but his gaze gave me a chill. It was almost like he could read my mind, like I was the one who caused the accident when I said that the two of them must watch out before something bad happens.

I could not have been the only one thinking that they were riding recklessly. But somehow, at that moment, I felt very responsible. As I gazed back at him, I wondered why he was not hurt as well. *What really happened?* I thought to myself. I asked a lady standing by. She said that a car pulled out of the parking space just as the young lad sped by. The lad tried to avoid the car by making a sharp turn. But when he turned, he turned right into an oncoming vehicle. It seemed that no one was paying attention. I asked her, *What about the other person riding with him?* She said, "What other person?"

I froze and the blood ran out of my body as though I was about to be hit by a vehicle. The shock of what she said sent me into a dazed state. At the time, it all seemed so surreal. I shook my head rapidly and said, *What do you mean what other person?* As I turned to point to the missionary, I said, *The young man right there*, but he was gone.

By this time, the police had arrived and began to push the crowd back out of the way. *What happened to the other guy?* I yelled! No one answered. Some people just looked at me and went in another direction. As the police tried to get the crowd under control, I pushed myself toward one of the officers. *Officer, officer,* I said. *There were two men here. What happened to the other man?*

"Ma'am, there is only one on the ground. Maybe the other is okay. I am sure he will fill us in on the details. Do not worry yourself. Just stand back and let the medics do their work," said the officer.

I looked everywhere, but I did not see the missionary. There was something very strange going on. *He will not get away with this,* I mumbled. These so-called missionaries were definitely hiding something. They were always around but never really helping. Once trouble happened, they disappeared. So I decided that on the following day, I would go to the police station to follow up on the matter. I believed that it was time to make people accountable for their responsibilities. The missionary knew exactly what happened, plus he may have even caused the problem. He forgot that I had a good description of him, and I would make sure the police knew everything when I got off from work. Right now I will go home and get my thoughts together. That way, when police asked me questions, I will have all the answers.

At the Police Station

As soon as I got off work the next day, I headed straight to the police station. Luckily, I was able to speak with the officer in charge. I told him that I had some information valuable to the bicycle accident that happened downtown yesterday about 5:15 p.m. I began to explain how there were two young men riding together. I told him that I did not actually see the accident but that when I went to the site, one of the men riding left the scene. I explained to him that I thought the man was from a missionary group, the one that is always around assisting people. The officer was not directly familiar with the group. I tried to describe them as much as I possibly could. As I was talking, I thought to myself that people were so self-consumed. They did not seem to pay attention to anything unless it involved them directly. I questioned how it was that I noticed people more than others, especially the police.

I also thought back to my earlier experiences with the church and some of my family members. I finally admitted that due to my own disappointments, I had subconsciously developed a dislike for the church and some people. Even though I had a pleasant experience at the revival, it still was not enough to totally change my perspective on things. The way I saw family members fight over material possessions but not lift a finger to take out a bag of dirty bed pads damaged my view of human nature. I began to think that I had too much hope in the missionaries. Somehow, I thought their work would change mankind. But they were people too and therefore not perfect. Yep, they were human just like the rest of us, prone to make mistakes.

After I finished talking, the officer thanked me for my information. He said that he would keep everything I told him in consideration. However, at the moment he did not feel the need to investigate further. He explained that several people present gave their recount of what happened. When he said that, I eagerly sat up with anticipation, believing that someone else had a similar story. But my excitement was short lived. There were five people who came forward. None of them mentioned a second bicyclist. One person did say that there were others out riding, but none with the young man who was hurt. That information did give me a gleam of hope. I felt that one witness was more focused than the other witnesses, just not as much as me. So I thanked the officer for allowing me some of his time.

It still puzzled me how some people could go so unnoticed. I still believed that there was more to the missionaries than what was known. I plotted secretly to get to the bottom of things. So I began to take matters in my own hands and do my own investigation.

THE NEIGHBOR

The next day was my day off, so I woke up early because I wanted to begin my day while it was still young. I went outside to get the newspaper when I saw my neighbor working in her garden. Alongside her was a missionary. I stared and thought for quite some time before I closed the door. I wondered to myself if I should approach my neighbor about her helper. This neighbor and I had not had the best relationship. She fussed when anyone got too close to her grass, flowers, or anything in fear that he or she would damage something. When I say anyone, I mean just that, "anyone". The paper and mail deliverers had a special box. No, a special box is not strange. It is just that the newspaper box and the mailbox were located at the end of the driveway, embedded in a distinctive casing of cement. This was to clearly identify where the newspaper and mail were to go and to keep anyone from stepping on the grass. When she came outside, she checked everything to make sure things were always in place. I would not have been surprised if she had cameras to survey the property, not for thieves, but for people and animals that stepped on her grass. Each time

I walked past, she always told me to be careful because she remembered the time I stumbled and fell on her lawn. I believed that she had an alarm that sounded each time I left my home. Because when I did, she would dash out her front door like she was running for the decathlon. Nevertheless, as ornery as I thought she was, I believed she could help me obtain the information I needed on the missionaries. I preferred to ask her after the missionary left, so I kept glancing at the two of them while I ate my breakfast.

A couple of people passed by, being very mindful of where they stood, stopped to talk with her. Seeing others converse with her helped build my confidence to approach her. Maybe she was not as bad as what I had made her out to be. I just had to be very nice and overlook her potential antics. Oh yes, she is a "screamer". How could I forget to mention that she yelled when she talked? At first, I thought she was hard of hearing, so I screamed as well. Then she told me that I was rude for hollering at an old lady. She wanted to know who or what raised me. So now I knew that she was a loud speaker. Boy, I hated to hear her when she was yelling.

More and more time passed as I watched and waited. I sat by the window so long that I almost fell asleep. I decided to confront her regardless of whether the missionary was there or not. *What do I have to be afraid of?* I thought to myself. So out the door I went. As I approached my neighbor's yard, the missionary looked my way, gently got up, and began to walk off. Once again, this grabbed me strangely. It was almost as though she knew I was coming to talk about her. Nevertheless her walking away worked out just fine. I really did not want to speak in front of her.

When I reached my neighbor, I made sure I did not step on anything but the sidewalk. I said, *Good morning!*

"Good morning to you," she replied.

Hmm, maybe this will work out fine after all, I whispered. So this built my courage even more as I moved forward into deeper waters of communication. I started off by saying; *Your yard is always so beautiful. I often watch you to get a few pointers for myself. I plan to start with something small in my yard like a few rose bushes until I get the hang of things. This will be a big step for me because gardening frightens me to death.* Then I chuckled.

Before I could get another word out, she interrupted me by saying, "It is about time. I was hoping you would take more care of the way your yard looks. You know that your yard is an extension of yourself. No one really knows what goes on in your home. But by looking at the outside of your home, it says a possibility of many things. It could be saying that you do not care about your surroundings. It may be saying that you keep your yard like you keep yourself." When she said that, it was the only time she stopped to look directly at me. Then she shook her head and looked back down.

After her glance, she continued to talk, but I did not hear a word she said. I just began to think that it was a waste of my time talking to her. If I had known that this would be her opportunity to insult me, I would not have bothered her. I would have taken a chance and spoken directly to the missionary. While my own thoughts were running through my head, I heard a loud, high-pitched, screechy voice saying, "Not only is your yard screaming for a new owner, but when I ask you a question, you rudely ignore me! If you are going to be so disrespectful, you can leave! I do not have to waste my time trying to help you!"

Oh no, this is what she sounds like when she is yelling, I thought.

Disguising my anger as best as I could, I said, *Oh my, I am so sorry, I just remembered I have to be somewhere. I did not mean to ignore you.*

My response seemed to have calmed her down. She went on to say, "Okay, well at least tell me what you wanted to know about the yard."

Well, I saw one of the missionaries helping you with the gardening and I wanted to know how I could get in touch with their group. They seem to be willing to work with just about anyone. I smiled as much as I could, trying very hard not to appear phony, to keep her at ease.

As I looked at her, she just stared at me as though I was speaking a foreign language. "What are you talking about?" she said. "What missionary, what group, what is wrong with you? Are you on some type of drug? If so, I do not want you coming over here. You are up to something. You are not looking for help. You probably want to steal from me and over here to see what you can get. I knew something was wrong with you. That is why you cannot keep your yard up. You are strung out." Then she yelled,

"Get away from me! I will be watching you! If I have any trouble at my house, you can best believe that I will send the police straight to your house!"

I dashed off as quickly as possible, not really understanding what had happened. *What did she mean what missionary? Did I mistake her friend to be someone else? Or am I as crazy as what the neighbor thinks that I am? If that was her friend, why did she walk off?* While I tried to think things through, I saw another missionary standing and staring at me. I was off to a bad start but determined to get to the bottom of things. So I approached her and said, *Hello.*

"Hello," she replied, but I quickly cut her off.

Do not talk. I told her. *I want to say what I have to say first, and then you can answer.* I went right into her. I had been polite long enough but still I was no further than when I began. I felt that there was no more room for tiptoeing around the subject.

What group do you belong to? Where do you all meet? Why do you help some people and not others? I went on and on, and after a while I said, *Okay, now it is your turn to talk.* The missionary hesitated. *Answer me!* I yelled. *I have had just about all I can take from you people.*

She stood there and with a gentle smile replied, "I cannot tell you what you want to know. It is not for me to say." Then she began to walk away.

Come back here! I demanded. *You will answer me or I will follow you all day! You will have to go home sometime. And if you go to the police that will be fine with me!*

Suddenly I felt a tap on my shoulder. It was a police officer. *Officer, officer!* I yelled. *I am so happy to see you. I want you to arrest this lady. She and her group are hiding something. They are behind something sinister, I just know it.*

"Calm down and come with me," he said.

But officer, she is getting away, I replied.

"No she is not," he said. "She will meet us at the office."

Finally I thought that I was going to get some answers.

THE DISCUSSION ROOM

When we arrived at the station, I spoke with the same officer who handled the bicycle incident. He escorted me to the discussion room. On the way there, I passed a lady in a striped shirt and jeans. Once in the room, he asked me if I knew why I was there. I told him about my confrontation with the missionary. He then asked me if I recognized the lady who was sitting in the hallway just before I entered the room. I said, no. He explained that she was the one who called the police because I was walking and hollering down the street. She thought I was dangerous. I told the officer that I was talking to a missionary who was a different lady and this lady had to have seen her.

The officer asked me to wait in the room for a while. About ten minutes later, he returned. He said he spoke with her, and that she only saw me. He explained that he had described the missionary to her but she denied seeing anyone who fit that description. My head began to spin. Everything I encountered that day was too much for me. I broke down, sobbing hysterically. *Why won't anyone believe me?* I shouted. *Why?* The officer would not let me leave right away. He was afraid I would hurt myself.

There was a room in the back with a padded mattress, blanket, and pillow. He led me there so I could rest and get myself together. I was not under arrest, but he just wanted me to rest first. However, he did say that there was a therapist available if I needed to talk to someone more deeply. Also, I was offered something to eat and a ride home if I desired. Right then I just wanted to rest, so that was exactly what I did.

After an hour or two of sleep, I got a cup of coffee and requested to go home. I assured the officer that I was okay and did not need a therapist. He gave me his number just in case I needed to reach him or if I changed my mind about the therapist.

Upon leaving the station, I saw the speaker from the revival. He saw me too and flagged me over. I was surprised he even recognized me since there were so many people there that night. He was not exactly the person I wanted to see. So when I went over to talk with him, it was more out of respect for who he was. Plus, I was impressed that he remembered me. This decision turned out to be the best one I made all day.

Meeting the Speaker

With the same echoing voice that captivated me before, he said, "Hello. I thought that was you. I am the minister from the recent park revival. You attended one of the church revival nights. I remember you because you seemed so out of place initially, but by the time you left, you were all into the service."

I politely smiled and said, *Yes that was me.*

"Which way are you going?" he asked. "Are you walking or driving? Me, I am just taking a slow stroll to my next destination. If you are going my way, I would love to have someone to talk to. We could take our time, talk, and before we know it, we will be at our destinations. I am not in a hurry, so I can accompany you and then go on to my stop."

I told him where I was going, and amazingly we were going the same way. So I agreed. Even though I was still not into church like he was, I felt that he would be a nice presence to have walking along beside me. So we walked and talked.

He began the conversation by asking me if I liked the revival. I told him that he was correct when he said at first I was a little uncomfortable. I explained that I was uncomfortable because I did not attend church except for weddings and funerals. Yet I did enjoy the service. I even thought about returning to church. But I was honest with him that I had some ill feelings regarding church people.

He asked me to elaborate. I did, and each time I expressed a concern, he understood but gave me a different way of looking at the situation. For example, I told him that some of the nastiest people I had ever met said that they were spiritual. They would curse at you. And later they would want to pray for you. *Who wants someone to pray for them after the person has been so nasty?* I asked.

He said, "Once a person has surrendered his or her life to God, God begins to work on that person. Many times God works on the underlying problem that causes people to be so nasty. This usually is not evident to anyone but the person God is working on. Sometimes even the nasty person does not realize that he or she is nasty. These people have been that way so long that they have convinced themselves that they are right. The church is like a hospital. People are somewhat like onions. They have layers and layers that make them who they are. Some onions are sweeter than others. An onion can look good but have bad spots. Some are just about rotten. But people differ from onions because God repairs people. He knows what needs to be done with each person to bring out their best, regardless of how rotten they seem. It is the responsibility of others to pray for people that they will grow as God leads them. Plus we must remember that no one is perfect. When we see bad things in others, others see bad things in us."

I thought deeply about each comment he made. Mostly, I appreciated how he let me vent. After about 30 minutes of venting, I came to the subject that I really wanted to talk about—the missionaries. I asked him what he thought about people whose job is to help but do not. They were present but when something really happens, they do nothing. He asked me if I was talking about anyone in particular, like he already knew what I was hinting at.

Since you asked, I said, there are some people who are always around assisting people with different things. I am not sure what the name of their organization is, so I just call them missionaries. They range in different ages, usually very close to the age of the person they are assisting. They seem to dress similar to the person as well.

He asked if any were at the revival. I said, Yes. He then asked if one was an usher who kept staring at me. I was not sure about the usher, so I said, *Maybe. There was an usher who seemed to stare.* At that moment he stopped, looked at me, and held my hand.

"I hope you do not mind me holding your hand," he said. "You have just asked a very dear question, and I want to give you as clear and caring answer as I possibly can."

Even though I was a little uncomfortable, I said, No, I *do not mind.*

İt İs Time

⸺≈⸺

He began saying, "I wondered if you noticed them. I believed that you did because it was not a coincidence we met at the police station. God told me to meet you here. It was time for me to explain your gift. I was not sure how to bring it up, however I do know that regardless of how difficult addressing certain conversations seem, it is always better to obey God."

As he was talking, I began to shake. I know he could feel me shaking because he asked me if I was okay. I trembled out a yes but also told him that when he started talking about my gift, he made me nervous. I went on to say, *This was why I was so into to your message. It just felt like you were talking directly to me. I deeply desire to be happy. I need to know what my gift is. I want to be fulfilled.* When I said that, he just smiled.

He said, "Well, you were one of the people God had me focus on. The usher was I guess you could say, assigned to you. That is why she seemed to focus on you. Her staring made you too nervous to leave, which was a good thing. You staying allowed you to hear what God wanted you to hear. In order for you to be happy, a seed had to be planted in you. Yes, you desire to be fulfilled, and God wants you to be happy! Therefore, God sent the seed through the message.

Nothing happened that evening by accident. You were overwhelmed and needed to walk. The music played, and you were drawn to it. The usher stared so you could not leave. The word of God was planted in your ear, buried in your heart, and later fertilized by what you have been going through. Now I am here to help guide you."

When I heard that, I yanked my hand back and began to walk away. I was not nervous anymore; I was frightened. *How did you know all of that?*, I said as I was walking away. *Who are you? Are you some kind of spy or the devil?*

He never moved but pleaded for me to come back. "Why do I have to be something bad? Why can't I be someone good who wants to help you?" he cried.

I stopped and turned around. With tears flowing and shaking like an earthquake, I said, *I will come a little closer. But do not touch me anymore, please.*

He agreed. He softly said, "First hear me out before you close me off." I nodded.

THE GIFT REVEALED

H e went on to say, "You can tell the difference between God and the devil. If you are experiencing something and later it is revealed to you what you have experienced, it is from God. God wants us to be knowledgeable. The devil wants us to be confused. But to have a better understanding, you must attend a good teaching church, pray, and study. Last but not least, you must be obedient to God's word." At that point he handed me a card with his church information on it.

What about the missionaries and why was the usher assigned to me? I asked.

He said, "Yes, they are like missionaries. They are angels assigned for different reasons. See, you have 'a gift of sight.' You can see in the spirit realm. You can see what others cannot. You can even converse with them, but you must learn how. This will fully come by a method called fasting and praying. The angels look like regular people so that they will not frighten the person who sees them." As he said these things, I thought about the missionary I was chasing in the street. I could see her but the people thought I was going insane.

He continued to say, "You have seen them all of your life. You have thought that they were good because they visited the sick, like your mother. People dying can often see them. This is why they stare off; they are looking at the angels." At this point I was crying almost uncontrollably. I knew I must pull myself together. For the first time in my life, what he is saying finally made sense.

He also said, "You have been disappointed because you felt they could do more. The angels you see cannot interfere with the future. They cannot prevent anything from happening. They are present to indicate that something is about to happen, like the boy on the bike. In the case of your mother, the angel was there to comfort her and escort her to her new home. You can see them because you have been assigned to help the people with their needs.

Now let's take your neighbor, for example. You saw an angel in the garden with her. Your neighbor is very sick, but she does not know how sick she really is. She knows that she has been feeling funny, but she has been ignoring it. If you had talked with the angel, she would have told you what was wrong."

Why did she leave as I was approaching? I asked.

He said, "You had not received the teaching you needed; therefore, you would not have understood. This," referring to the teaching, "is what you are getting now. You must go to your neighbor, look past her outward demeanor, and in some manner convince her that she needs to check on her health. I cannot tell you what to say or how to deliver the information. This is why you must pray and meditate for God to show you the best approach."

·Oᴎᴇ ᴍᴏʀᴇ Tʜɪᴎɢ

"**O**h, I almost forgot. Before all of this takes place, there is one more thing you must do—the most important part. You must totally surrender your heart to God. Let God be the head of your life."

Why? I asked. *I still have the gift, don't I?*

"Many people have a gift," he replied. "Some use their gift to lead people the wrong way. This is why so many people are hurt and do not want anything to do with God. Therefore it is better to be under God's direction and protection. These things plus more God gives you when you surrender to Him.

I believe you will be different. Your heart is filled with love and compassion. And if you believe what I have said about you and the angels then believe me now. You must be led by God to be effective.

I will warn you that there will be people who will challenge you. You will know that their spirit is not from God. God will tell you what to do each time. There will be times when it will seem as though these people will have the upper hand. But this is never true. Anyway, do not worry about all of this now. These things will be worked out, first things first.

You must surrender to God. Will you do that with me now?"

Yes, I replied. Right then we bowed our heads and prayed. He asked me if I believed. After I said yes, he asked me to repeat some words after him. I did. As he was praying, I felt a sense of peace like never before. Everything seemed much clearer, not weighty like before. A warm tingling feeling ran up and down my body.

When he finished praying, I looked up and there was the missionary—I mean angel—whom I was chasing in the street. She smiled and said she would always be near to comfort and protect me whether I see her or not. She patted me on the shoulder as she walked away. The minister said she was my guardian angel and that God has one assigned to everybody. Of course I was glad to hear that.

He then asked me if he would see me in church Sunday. I nodded. "One more thing" he said. "You and I are still human. We still have the same obstacles to face as everyone else. Some days you will feel good and some days you will not. Yet God will always make a way for you to get your job done. Now go away thanking and praising God, and don't forget to use your gift!"

With a big hug, I squeezed him, and then kissed him on the cheek.

I ran off smiling, crying, and waving.

Conclusion

As I approached home, I saw my neighbor and the angel. When I walked up, the angel stood and said, "Welcome." I just smiled because I did not want the neighbor to think that I was crazy.

Good evening, I said as I passed by.

"I hope it is a good evening," she replied. Never looking up, she went on to say, "I do not want anymore trouble out of you."

Oh you won't, I replied. *I was thinking about what you said, and you were so right.*

"Good" she replied, still not looking at me.

Well my plan is to do better, I told her. I also said that, *I hoped you are taking care of yourself as well as you are taking care of your garden. You know that there is only one you, and your garden needs you.*

That time, she turned around and stared at me. "Funny you said that," she replied. "I have been feeling a little funny and was wondering what was going on. Maybe I will call the doctor before it gets too late."

Yes, do that. I replied. *It is always better to find out than to assume.* I ended the conversation by saying, *Okay, have a nice day, and do not forget to call the doctor.*

"I won't, and thank you," she said in a tender and appreciative voice.

At that time the angel smiled, got up, and walked away. I guess that was the sign that my neighbor would do what she said she would do, or that I had done what I was suppose to have done. I chuckled because it felt good to talk with my neighbor and not have her holler at me. And for her to say thank you was priceless. Wow, I knew this had to be from God! But I kept in mind what the minister first said at the revival. Each time would not be easy, but I knew it would be worth it. And even though this was just the beginning for me, I did feel fulfilled.

Though years have passed, I have spoken to many people in many places about many things. The faces have changed, but some things remain the same. I am helping people! It is not always easy. However, I am fulfilling my purpose in life. And yes it is true, I am satisfied and I am happy! Thank you, God, for my gift!

THE TRIP

Introduction: The Trip

—∞—

A couple loves to sightsee. So one year after visiting some family members, the two decide not to rush back home but wander off a little. They see a sign where a bed and breakfast offers ferry rides. Both of them believe that this would be nice detour. But as it is well known, things are not always as nice as they seem. Luckily the wife takes the advice of an elderly lady. This advice just may save their lives.

It is Final

W̶ith my voice trembling and my body frozen with fright, *No Kevin!* I yell. But he doesn't listen to me. He just shakes his head and says, "Calm down, you're overreacting again."

I clutch his arm, yank, and pull it as I plead with him to believe me. He does all he can to stay focused on the road. "Let me go!" he firmly insists. "Just stop it! I made my decision and it is final!"

I let go and sit back, tightly gripping each side of my chair. Extremely frightened, I stare, watching every sign while Kevin smiles and pats my hand. Slowly we turn and enter in. I can't help but think back to the night before we left to visit the family.

Thinking about the Trip

I was so excited. I looked forward to seeing my husband's side of the family. They are just some of the nicest people you ever want to meet. Plus I love that they live in a rural area, far away from heavy traffic and the constant hustle and bustle of everyday life. This is not to say that the people do not work hard. Quite to the contrary, they work very hard. It is just a different type of life there. Most people are factory workers, farmers, or crop owners. Because of their employment, many of the houses are spaced several acres apart, sometimes separated by marshes and swamps. The space also allows plenty of room to party and reminisce without disturbing the neighbors.

From where we live, it is just as easy to drive as it is to fly. The closest airport is in the metropolitan area, but that is miles away from where his family lives. When we drive, we travel a nice scenic route of mountains, bodies of water, wooded areas, and fields. It is not unlikely to see a family of deer grazing and a wide variety of birds flying or wading in the water.

Also along the way there are several rocky or dirt roads, extensions off the main highway, which seems to lead into the horizon. Each of the roads is labeled with a route number. Some indicate that they offer access to other facilities, such as gas stations, rest areas, restaurants, etc. Most of the mailboxes are located at the main highway junction. I often wondered how far the homeowners or proprietors have to travel just to get their mail. My husband and I frequently talked about venturing onto one of those roads to see where it leads.

There is one road that has a sign advertising ferryboat rides. So this year after leaving the family, we decided to veer off on this road. The sign also indicated that they offer carriage rides, a bed and breakfast, and tennis courts. They claimed to have the most eloquent and comfortable bed and breakfast in that part of the state. We love to sightsee. And being that we generally take one vacation a year, we try to get the most of out it. Our plan was to leave early Wednesday morning.

If we left around 5 a.m., we should reach the family's home no later than 9 p.m. Wednesday night. This was providing that we only stop for gas and a couple of light meals. We usually stopped for lunch around 11 a.m. and dinner around 4 p.m. By the time we arrived, most of the family would be asleep. So all we would have to do is to unpack and settle down for a well-deserved good night's rest.

The next day would give us an opportunity to greet everyone, catch up on old times and finish preparing the meals. On Friday, there would be a huge family picnic. This was always fun. They would have a pit barbeque, fried fish (fish caught fresh from a day or two before), and a variety of entrees, side dishes, and desserts. Everyone chipped in and brought his or her specialty. Mine is carrot cake. I prefer to make them a few hours before we leave so they will be nice and fresh when we arrive. Plus I fix it at home because I do not want to fully share my recipe. The preparation for the trip and the long drive really takes a toll on us, so we really look forward to a good night's sleep before the barbeque.

The house we will be staying in belongs to my husband's aunt. She says she can always tell when we are close by because she can smell the cakes a mile away. She is the matriarch of the family. She is a short, middle-weight lady somewhere in her early nineties. For her age, she looks great. She is barely gray and needs no assistance except for a cane. Her specialty is the lemonade and iced tea, plus she oversees the picnic. Everyone has the utmost respect for her. Even though she has taught the family how to cook many of the dishes, she still gives her opinion if she feels we are falling behind on our techniques. She will tell you quick that she may be getting older, but that only means her taste buds are becoming more refined. So when she feels that our food is not up to par, she will also let us know what's missing.

Cooking is one thing my husband's family and my family have in common. Our recipes have been passed down from generation to generation. They are judged on taste and presentation. The techniques used can not completely be put down on paper. For us, cooking is a personal experience. It is something that only the five senses can determine, and therefore the method goes far beyond the pages of a cookbook. Nevertheless, mishaps are bound to happen from time to time. If they do, it only becomes a joke among us, and no one takes any comments to heart.

Also at the picnic, we will play games, dance, and as the night moves in, we catch up by telling stories over an outdoor fire. To me this is almost the best part of the day. It gives each of us a chance to relax after a full day of excitement. If there are any lingering ill feelings, we will clear them up there. We will let each other know how much we appreciate them. Everyone starts fresh, never to discuss the matter again. My husband's aunt reminds us constantly that tomorrow is not promised, so forgive today.

Saturdays are great too. Every year the state has a big fair that runs from Friday to Sunday. Saturday is the biggest event day. Once again I looked forward to tasting the locals' festive treats. I enjoy the costumes and songs that tell the history of the land. But I have to admit that I love the vendors the most. They seemed to stream along each side of the road a mile or two. You can buy anything from livestock to already prepared meals, carved crafts, crafted right on site, herbs, clothing, jewelry, and mud body massages. I haven't had to nerve to try one of those yet.

Usually after a day at the fair, my husband and I will return to his aunt's house. Since we decided to take the ferryboat ride, we will part ways at the fair. The bed and breakfast is about a two-hour ride from the fair, but we believed that it would be well worth the time. His aunt's house is about an hour drive from the fair, so we thought we could last another hour. All we wanted to do was to get there safely. Once we checked in, we would sleep until morning.

Sunday would be our way to relax and have fun at the same time before our long journey home. We would sleep over and plan to arrive home Monday night. This would give us all day Tuesday to rest before returning to work Wednesday. Now I pray that everything goes as planned.

☉n ☉ur Way

The weather was perfect for driving that day. Even though the drive was long, getting away helped ease the tension. The talking, laughing, singing, and sightseeing helped the time go a lot faster. My husband is always the designated driver. I drive sometimes, but he is the primary one. He says driving relaxes him, but I really don't think he likes female drivers, especially me. I am always playing tricks on him, and he is afraid I will do it while I am driving. He doesn't like any horsing around on the road. Nevertheless, it doesn't bother me. We make a perfect team. He loves to drive, and I love to ride.

I remembered when we reached the sign to the ferry rides. I jumped up and down as I said that I couldn't wait until we stopped there. Even though we visited his family frequently, this would be the first time we ventured somewhere without them. To me this was going to be my well-deserved, overdue second honeymoon.

At the Aunt's House

As scheduled, we reached his aunt's house about 9 p.m. She lives in a small town where the houses look like huge cottages hidden in the woods. Just about everyone is kin. She lives with her daughter, her daughter's husband, and their two children, her son, and his four children. The son's wife died before I had a chance to meet her. When we arrived, he was waiting to welcome us. The rest of the family was sleep because everyone tries to get up early to prepare for the picnic. So we quietly carried everything upstairs and went to bed.

Thursday morning we awoke to the smell of fresh-brewed coffee, country ham, eggs, grits, and warm sticky buns. Much chattering was coming from outside of our bedroom window. My husband looked out and yelled that we would be down shortly. He then told me that a lot of folks were here to see us. Some of them we had not spoken to since our last year's visit. I love all of them, but some of them I can't wait to see. One is Uncle Lee. He tells the funniest stories. The things most people take serious, he has a way of turning it into a comedy. Also, I love how he sits. Anytime he tells a story, he leans over, places his elbows on his knees, rocks, and claps his hands as he animates each version. He will have your sides aching before the day is over. Throughout the day, he enjoys picking with us. His wife is funny too. She is forever saying,

"Lee, why don't you hush your lying?"

He'll just say, "I ain't lying, baby. I'm just telling it like I see it. Some folks see it one way. This is my way." Then he just goes back to where he left off before she interrupted him.

There is Aunt Julie. She is not blood kin but she has been a friend to the family all of her life, so she is just like family. She likes to go from person to person collecting and carrying the town's gossip while telling the most fascinating stories. If she hears something juicy, you will always know it because you can hear her say, "You don't say," from wherever she is. This year I even got caught up in her conversation.

She was thrilling us with tales of missing tourists. She said, "Some of the people have made up a chant." She began to hum a tune to these words: "They come from all parts of the land to see-our mountains, our rivers, and our many trees-but what they get, they never planned for-their picture on a poster, possibly murdered, shucks, no one knows for sure-so if you plan to visit us here, take this little advice-don't go anywhere by yourself, unless you like gambling with your life."

She told me that my husband and I did not have to be afraid. The people missing were new to the area; and people who snatch people only snatched those who did not have connections here. My husband warned me not to fall for her stories because many people have gotten in trouble believing her.

Then there is cousin Birdie. She is a heavy drinker, and she starts early. Yet she is a lot of fun. She stumbles her way around, picking with everyone. She loves to belch out songs as she tries to get someone to dance. The children have a ball with her. The grown-ups try to get her to sit down and sober up. Sometimes she will for a minute or two. The longest time is when she falls to sleep. When she wakes up, she appears as though she doesn't know where she is, plus she is very quiet. But that does not last long. It may take her some time to remember, but she never forgets where the booze is. After a couple of sips, she is right back to her normal state—drunk.

These are just a few of them. We all know that each of us is different in our own way, so we respect that. We get along very well and pride ourselves on teaching our children to be the same way.

GETTING READY
FOR THE PICNIC

M ost of Thursday my husband spent his time reminiscing and working with the men, and I did the same with the women. I helped get things ready and watched the parade of new dresses acquired since the last time we were together. The ladies wanted to know everything from my job to whether my husband had considered moving back there. This was his hometown, and I admitted that the thought had crossed his mind. *Maybe when he retires*, I told them. My husband is the captain of the police department and only has a few more years to go before he retires. As for me, I am a manager and would not mind a change of environment, possibly a change of career.

Then the ladies began to say that if we did move, there would be someone who would be with us at all times to familiarize us to the area. They stressed how important it was that everyone knew we had roots here. I chuckled and said, Yep, *I got that impression from Aunt Julie. I don't want to gamble with my life.*

They smiled but stared at me solemnly. I even hummed the words, hoping to break the icy glare, but I realized that I should not have made a joke out of the matter. Gratefully, one of the ladies broke the silence by saying, "Let's not talk about this anymore. We're going to scare her before they even decide if they're going to move." I was glad the conversation changed yet wondered what was really going on here. Surely we were not being told all there is to know.

Picnic Day

Friday was all we had hoped it to be and more. Everyone did a great job. I jumped rope with the young girls and almost drowned trying to bob for apples. My husband and I tried our luck at the three-legged potato sack race as well as a nice, friendly game of hearts. When the evening came, we all gathered by a warm campfire. It is pretty warm during the day here, but as the night falls, with all the trees around, it gets a little cool. So a campfire is just a perfect way to end the day. This year we did something a little different, or at least it was the first time that I have seen it. Last year we lost a couple of family members, a husband and wife. Both of them were well into their eighties. The wife died first and husband died a few days after. We have always believed that if two people really loved and thrived on each other, when one of them passes, the other will soon follow. This was another example of that belief.

That evening we gave tribute to them. Each of us shared a particular story about them that was close to our hearts. Their children, all in their upper forties and early fifties, wept as we reminisced. That night before my husband and I went to sleep, we hugged and expressed how much we really appreciated each other. I fell asleep in his arms and cried as I thought about how blessed I was to be a part of this great family.

Saying Goodbye
to the Aunt

aturday morning came, and that meant a full day at the fair. Some of the family went along as well. They owned an old school bus; so whenever a lot of them needed to travel together, they would use the bus. They would pile as many as they could inside and hit the road. From the outside the bus looked a little worn, but it ran smooth and purred like a kitty cat.

As much as I was looking forward to the bed and breakfast the next day, I was also saddened to know that our family gathering was just about over. I cannot stress enough that I really enjoy these people, especially my husband's aunt.

His aunt decided not to go with us this year. She said it was too much walking for her. We told her that we had definitely decided to stay at the bed and breakfast, so we would not be returning from the fair. She said that she was shocked to hear that the establishment was still in business. A few years back, there had been a lot of publicity over the death of the owner's wife. He was thought to have killed her, but it was never proven. She said that she used to clean the bed and breakfast nook and that the whole family was a little strange. The wife was different than the rest of them. She wasn't from around here, and his children were not hers. His aunt did not know who their real mother was, but it was rumored that they were a product of incest.

There are four children in all, two boys and two girls. One daughter, the youngest, is mentally unstable. All of the children look very similar, like they could be quads. The owner has a sister and had a brother who went missing years ago. The owner and his sister also look similar, and it is believed that his children may be hers. She is mentally challenged as well but not as much as the daughter. The bed and breakfast sits on an old family plantation that is about twelve acres in size. Before the death, they used to do a lot of business. So she just reminded us by saying "Just be careful, and let them know who your family is."

My husband said okay. But from listening to her and remembering what Aunt Julie said, I wasn't sure if stopping there was a good idea. My husband asked her if anything else suspicious had happened. She said no, but what Aunt Julie said the day before did have some truth to it. Several of the local towns had reported an occasional missing person. None of them had been found, and the disappearances had not been directly linked to that place. But when you are by yourself, you have to be extra careful. Since nothing was linked to the establishment, my husband felt that we should still keep our original plans. As for me, I still wasn't sure. I couldn't get out of my mind how the ladies got quiet. My husband went on to say that if it did not seem like a place we wanted to stay when we got there, then we would just come back to the family house. I agreed and promised to call his aunt to let her know what we decided.

A Day at the Fair

At the fair, there seemed to be more food vendors than what I remembered. I surprised myself that I could eat so much after Friday's barbeque. Along with tasting some of the finest cuisine, I blew fire with one of the fire-breathing performers and made a glass vase with one of the local craftsmen. Of course, mine did not look as good as the ones he made.

There was an old Hungarian-looking lady who waved us over to her booth. She was selling medallions with stones found only in her native land. She wanted me to buy one and said that it would warn me of any danger. Even though I did not believe in such things, I bought one because she was so nice. She placed the medallion firmly in my hand and said, "Put it around your neck before you forget. You must wear it in order for it to protect you and your loved ones."

I asked her how I would know if it was working. She said it would light up. The medallion was deep orange with yellow- and cream- colored specks. She explained that when danger was near, the specks would glow. I nodded but did not quite understand. The specks were already shimmering. How could they glow anymore? I looked at her and she smiled and said, "You will know" as if she was reading my mind.

As we walked away, I asked my husband if he thought she was strange. He said no and felt that I had been spooked ever since Friday. He said people in this area believed and practiced a lot of things. This is one reason why he wanted to leave the area. And it was also why he had not fully decided if he wanted to move back after he retired. He was hoping that things would have changed. They had, but not enough.

Just before the sun began to set, we all decided it was a good time to leave. We had about an hour drive longer than the rest of the family. If we left now, we could arrive at the bed and breakfast before it got too late. We all hugged and promised to keep in touch. Then my husband and I headed toward our next destination.

On the Way to the Bed and Breakfast

Usually, I am pretty good company for my husband, but that night I was tired. He said he did not mind if I went to sleep, but I did not want to. Driving is always much easier if you have someone to help you stay alert. Regretfully, I did nod off a couple of times but managed to wake up shortly before our turn on the road to the bed and breakfast.

The first thing I saw was the brightly lit sign that said, "Ferry rides next right." As I looked at the sign, I also noticed that my medallion was glowing bright yellow. At first I thought the medallion was glowing from the reflection of lights. But once we passed completely under the sign, it was still glowing. I brought it to my husband's attention, and he figured it was like a mood ring he owned when he was young. Someone told him that the ring had the same special powers. Every time it changed colors, he feared the worst. Eventually he threw it away because it spooked him so bad. As for the medallion, it stayed lit all the way to the bed and breakfast. I slipped it inside my shirt because I did not want to spook any of the people there.

The road to the bed and breakfast was very narrow. It was supposed to be a two-lane road, but you have to drive very carefully. Both sides of the road were woody; one side has a swamp. At any given time, I feared something was going to run out in front of us.

At the Bed and Breakfast

Eventually we entered into a beautiful floral landscape with a lovely three-story cottage accented with balconies, water fountains, and a marble circular driveway. I saw a tennis court sitting somewhat behind the cottage and a ferry sitting a little ways off from the house. To left side of the house, there was a man putting away a couple of horses and another man coming off the porch. Both men looked to be in their upper thirties and had very similar facial features. Before I could say it, my husband said that they must be the two sons because they looked alike.

The man on the porch came to our car to greet us. "Welcome," he said. He seemed very friendly, and I began to feel a little more relaxed. When I looked down at my medallion, it had stopped glowing, and I felt that this was a good sign.

The gentleman introduced himself as Envil. He was tall and a little on the stocky side. He had a nice face and smile even though he did not have any teeth except for one gold tooth in the upper right part of his mouth. As he grabbed the luggage, he asked us how long we would be staying. "A day or two," my husband replied. We told him we were excited about taking a ferry ride. Envil grinned and said, "Fine, that will be just fine." I noticed that there were only two vehicles outside besides ours, a muddy pickup truck and a small red car with out-of-town license plates. So I asked him about the other guests. He said that business had been slow for a while but the family enjoyed what they did and did not want to give it up. I smiled and said that I understood completely.

As we were entering the hotel, the sheriff drove up. I had mixed feelings about that because I wondered if something was wrong. Hopefully he was just checking on the place. I was able to talk to myself positively, and decided that it was nice to have the sheriff stop by and check on the place. I needed to stop making every little thing into something negative.

Envil hollered and said, "Hi, sheriff." The sheriff just waved. The man who was with the horses came out and talked with the sheriff at his car as Envil escorted us inside.

Inside the Cottage

～～

We went inside to a softly lit, intricately decorated, huge, colonial-style room. There was a gorgeous metal staircase that led to the upstairs in a circular fashion. The registration desk looked hand carved because there were figures of people and flowers that ran along the main beams, each figure uniquely different. All of the wood looked mahogany. There were several marble-top tables with glass and brass figurines on them. The chairs were all wood except for the seating and backing which were covered in tapestries. The floor was a combination of white and black marble tile with a cream colored carpet that had green ivy which ran along its boarder. The whole room glistened to perfection. Whoever kept it clean did a spectacular job.

At the front desk was a thickly built lady who looked to be in her upper forties. She was dressed very casual in a cotton pullover shirt and jeans. Her hair was scraggily, and her face was very blank, as if she had little to no emotions. This had to be one of the sisters. She also looked very similar to the two men. If it wasn't for her female mannerisms, I would have mistaken her for a man.

She welcomed us in and explained about the room times, the breakfast time, and the ferry tour times. I asked her if the tour would run being that they did not have that many visitors. She simply said yes and then turned and glimpsed at an older man who was sitting in a chair in the darkest corner of the room. He did not say much, but he watched everything we all did. I asked if he was another guest. She said no; he was her father and the one who made all of the decisions. I should have known he wasn't a visitor because he looked like a farmer in his plaid shirt and bib-top jeans. He just sat there firmly focused and chewed on a piece of straw. I tried not to let his stare make me uncomfortable, so I smiled and looked through the huge double glass door just to the side of the chair he was sitting in. The landscape was gently lit with rope lighting along the paths and around the fixtures. I could not wait to see it in the morning.

The Medallion Comes On

B efore she gave us our key, she said her name was Millie and father's name was Papa Joe. If we needed anything, either of them would be happy to assist us. We thanked her and I turned to thank the father by waving my hand. As I did that, I felt a warm sensation on my chest. I looked down and saw the medallion light up but it went right back out. Millie asked, "What's with the glow?" I glanced at my husband and turned back to her, smiled, and said, *Oh, that's just my pager. I guess the family wants to make sure we arrived safely.*

To cover my tracks, I tried to use my cell phone, but it did not work. I asked Millie if there was a phone in our room. She said yes but there is also one right in the lobby if I needed to call right then. *That's okay*, I said. *I will just wait until we unwind upstairs.* Millie said she understood but told us that we must call home. She said, "Family gets very nervous when you don't keep in touch." Then she glanced at her father again.

I smiled at her and turned to smile at Envil and Papa Joe to make it seem as though I was not nervous and telling the truth. Even though I lied, it worked out perfectly because I wanted to let my husband's aunt know that we were here just in case.

Just as I was turning away from Papa Joe, I caught a brief glimpse of what seemed to be a lady peeking through the glass door. She moved too fast for me to really tell. I think it was a woman because it seemed as though she was wearing a dress. Trying not to obviously stare, I quickly looked down and acted as though I was still into the conversation about the family.

Unable to control myself, I again glanced toward Papa Joe. This time I was able to get a clearer view of the person, and it was a woman. She was in a dress, and her hair was white, rolled up on top of her head in a bun. But what I saw caused me to jerk. She was trying to restrain a young boy. One of her hands was around his mouth and the other around his chest. Then she yanked him away quickly. The only thing I noticed about the boy was that he had dark hair and wore a white shirt with flowers.

I knew I was staring a little too much, but I was trying to figure out why she was restraining the boy. Then I thought to myself that maybe he was her grandchild and she didn't want him to disturb us. My staring and being startled alarmed Papa Joe. He sat on the edge of the chair and turned to see what I was looking at. Once again, trying not to draw attention to myself, I said that the scenery looked beautiful; and that I couldn't wait to see it in the morning.

Here Comes the Sheriff

*S*uddenly and with a loud thump, the front door opened and I jumped again. Envil told my husband that I was either very nervous or easily spooked. My husband said that I was always like that when I was tired. I thought that was a good answer even though I knew my husband was really wondering what was wrong with me. I apologized and quickly agreed with my husband.

It did comfort me a little bit when I saw that it was the sheriff. "Sorry about the door, folks," he said. "The wind is picking up and it caught the door before I could. I didn't mean to let it slam like that."

Envil said, "Sheriff, you have to watch that. You're going to frighten away our only customer in over a week."

Over a week? I quietly mumbled. *When we were coming in, I saw a small red car with out-of-town plates. If the car belonged to one of them, why did it have out-of-town plates?* By this time, I wasn't feeling comfortable about staying at all. I didn't say anything at that moment. I could sense that the father was suspicious of me because he never took his eyes off me.

The sheriff said that he was sorry he had stopped by so late but there had been a report of a missing lady and her young son. He said earlier today he received a picture text message from one of the lady's friends she and her son was supposed to have met hours ago but they never showed. They were in a small red car. The friend said that the lady and her son were going to do some sightseeing before meeting up with the rest of the gang. She had mentioned that she might take a ferry ride and the sheriff wanted to know if any of us had seen her. He said that he had a long talk with Jake outside but he said he had not seen anyone who fit their description. Since he had seen us come in, he thought he would ask if we had seen them. My husband said that we had spent the day at the fair and he did not know if he would recognize anyone. I asked what they looked like. The sheriff said that the lady and the boy have brown hair. She is twenty-nine and the boy is eight. From the picture text, she was wearing a yellow sundress trimmed with daisies and the boy was wearing a white shirt with a dark blue floral pattern. At that time I tried not to let my eyes give my thoughts away by widening.

While the sheriff was talking, Papa Joe, never speaking, came closer to make sure he could hear what we were saying. My husband asked me if I remembered anyone who fit that description. I said no and that it is sad when people go missing. "By the way," the sheriff said. "Where are you people from?"

"Oh yeah," my husband said. "My aunt told me to tell you who our family is. She says it makes a difference when people know who you are a kin to. I am the youngest of Kitty Ranger's children."

"Kitty Ranger's boy, you say," said Envil. "Well goodness be. I remember your ma, pa, and all the young-ins. I know she moved away while ya'll were real little. I heard she and your pa died. Is that true?"

"Yes" my husband replied. "My daddy got a job in another county. Later, I moved to another state for a better education. After landing a good job and getting married, I decided it was time to revisit my roots. Since we have been coming back, we always wanted to take a ferry ride. This year we decided to stop."

"Well then, sheriff, they are just like family," Envil responded. "We do treat family folks different around here. Ain't that right, sheriff?"

"That's right" said the sheriff. Everyone smiled and nodded except Papa Joe.

Envil was the outspoken one of the family. I could understand why the family let him be the greeter. Jake and Papa Joe were standoffish. Millie did talk a little. Between me and my husband, he is the more outspoken one. As for me, I'm a little on the cautious side.

After hearing about the boy with the white floral shirt, I felt as though I swallowed a frog whole, and it was stuck in my throat. Before leaving, the sheriff thanked everyone for helping. He also said that he would be back the next day to put up posters along the highway and outside the cottage just in case someone had some information. Envil said that would be fine. My husband shook hands as I nodded my goodnight gestures. Then off to our room we went.

In the Room

Once in the room, I could not wait to tell my husband what I thought I saw. He told me that I should take the medallion off. He felt that it and all the stories were starting to get to me. I asked him if he noticed the red car parked beside the house. He said not really. I then asked him if he would go outside with me to see if the car was still there. He said if the car was there, then why didn't the sheriff see it? That was a good point he made. So I figured someone must have hid it, but I wondered how. It was there when we arrived and the sheriff came up soon after. Maybe the older lady moved it while we were not looking and that is why she was outside. Then I told my husband that I was pretty sure that was the missing boy I saw. I recognized the description of his shirt. "Enough already," he shouted. "You are over exaggerating again, and I am too tired for this tonight." I sighed and kept quiet.

My husband went to take a shower as I sat on the bed not sure of anything. I looked around and saw how lovely our room was. It was located in the back of the cottage with a view of the river. It had a cozy country feel with a queen-size canopy bed. The bed was so comfortable that I don't believe I have ever felt a mattress so firm but yet so soft. I leaned back and began to relax. As I glanced over at the double glass doors that led to the balcony, I thought I could use a breath of fresh air.

On the Balcony

⸺⸎⸺

I opened the door, stepped outside, and took a deep breath. With my head up and enjoying the breeze, I noticed a flash in the distance. It was coming from the direction of the river. I could not quite make out what it was, but it was something large sliding into the water. The moonlight caused the item to reflect in the night. Before it was totally submerged, it looked like the back end of a vehicle. As I stood there trying to figure out if it was a car or not, I saw someone near the item. I believed that whoever it was, was looking my way, but I wasn't sure. I didn't think to cut out the bedroom light before standing on the balcony.

When I saw the person, I quickly turned, ran inside and closed the balcony door. *Kevin, Kevin,* I whispered. *We must leave. I can't stay here. Something just doesn't feel right.* My husband came out and said, "Okay. We'll leave, but not now, only in the morning." I asked why not now. He said he was too tired to drive and he did not trust my driving. He felt that I was too upset, and afraid that I would drive us into the swamp. The last thing he wanted to happen was for us to become missing as well. I explained that I would not be able to sleep. He said that was my decision but he was going to bed.

A Knock at the Door

Just as he went to get into the bed, someone knocked on the door. It was Millie and her dad. "Everything all right?" she yelled.

My husband opened the door and replied, "Yes everything is great.

We were just getting ready to go to bed."

"Okay then," she said. "Let us know if you need anything."

"Okay, good night," he said and closed the door. I didn't say anything, and by that time I was too nervous to hide my fear. I knew that the father did not trust me. His eyes beamed on me as though he was trying to put me in a trance. The only thing I could do was to try and not stare at him.

I decided to take a shower but asked my husband if he could at least stay up until I came out. He agreed. After washing off, I jumped into the bed and snuggled him. I kept the medallion on but forgot to make the phone call.

We awoke about 6 a.m. in the morning. I freshened up first this time and decided to watch a little television while my husband was getting ready. I turned on the television set and there was a news report about the missing family. She was pretty with long dark brown hair, and a lovely smile. I could not help feeling sorry for her and her son. Then I saw something that accelerated my fear. She had a gold tooth in the upper right side of her mouth. Not wanting to start anything with my husband, I didn't say anything. I was just glad we were leaving even though I could smell a delicious breakfast waiting. I was willing to skip it just to get out of there.

Breakfast Time

───※───

When we arrived downstairs, all of the family along with two other women was in the dining room waiting for us. One of the women looked like the older lady I saw last night. Her hair was gray and up, and her face was extremely wrinkled. But it was her eyes and her smile that stood out the most. Her eyes were wide with excitement, and her mouth twitched as though she could not wait to speak, but she never did. The other lady was much younger but noticeably mentally challenged. Her head hung forward and to one side. She rocked back and forth, constantly looking up and giggling. When she saw us she said in a scratchy voice, "Visitors pa, visitors." Papa Joe angrily looked at her and said, "Hush, gal." As she spoke, I trembled.

"Good morning," Envil hollered. "We all been waiting for you. We didn't want to start breakfast without you."

I did not mind having something to eat, but I definitely did not want to sit down and eat with them. My husband replied, "Sorry, we didn't know you all were waiting on us." I was clutching his hand. He moved forward and I was frozen stiff. He ignored my gesture and yanked me to get started.

Introduced to the Rest of the Family

E nvil continued and said, "Well, this here is all my family. You met my brother, Jake, my sister, Millie, and my pa, Papa Joe. These two lovely ladies here are my aunt and sister. The older is my aunt T, that's short for Tessa, and the other is my sister Ceda. Her name is Ceda because our ma tripped over a cedar stump before she was born. So my dad said that we would call her Ceda."

Where's your mom" I asked. All of them, even my husband, turned and looked at me.

"Well," Envil explained, "she left this world early, praise be. You know that is some of our fates, to leave early. Some leave earlier than others."

"Earlier than others," Ceda said as she chuckled.

"Hush up, gal, don't let me tell you again," Papa Joe replied. I thought to myself that I knew what she was thinking. Speaking of leaving, if I was in control of things, we would have left last night.

Then Envil said, "Enough with all the conversation. We're hungry! Let's eat then talk." Envil asked my husband to say the grace, and he did. He thanked the family for the lovely food and for making us feel at home. He requested that their business would thrive again like they needed it to. We all said amen, but I prayed that if they had done anything wrong, they would get caught.

"How was your rest?" Millie asked.

"Great, just great," we both replied. My husband stated that it was the best night's sleep he had in a long time.

"You're just like kinfolk," Envil told my husband. "I hope we can do something to put you to rest little lady," referring to me. Ceda giggled and nodded her head a lot.

I'm fine. I'm never fully comfortable unless I'm home," I replied. My husband shouted out, "Amen to that." They all laughed, even me.

Trouble with the Car

After breakfast, Envil asked if we were ready for the ferry ride. My husband explained that we had decided to leave early and skip the ride. "That's a shame," Envil replied. "Since you were our only visitors, we had an extra-nice tour waiting for ya'll. But if you can't stay, you can't stay." So we packed everything in the car and said our goodbyes. Ceda and Aunt T walked off. Millie and Envil stayed with us at the car.

After getting in the car, my husband tried to start it, but the engine would not turn over. I whispered that they have done something to it since it had been working up to now. I told my husband that I hoped he finally believed me. Envil came over and asked, "What's the matter?"

"Don't know," my husband said. "It just won't start."

"Jake, come take a look at their car," Envil yelled. "He's a mechanic you know. He'll get it running for you good people." As Jake walked past, he stared at me. I decided to smile but this time stare and not look away. I wanted them to know I was on to what they were doing.

Jake popped open the hood quickly and immediately saw what the problem was, too quick if you ask me. "Something's loose, but I can fix it," he grunted.

Envil leaned over and said, "Since ya'll have to wait for your car, what about that ride? It will only take Jake a short time to fix it. By that time the ferry ride will be over, you folk can be on your way." My husband agreed. I, on the other hand, felt that they were up to no good. I did not believe that we were going to leave this place alive. So I threw out what I called a trump card, something that would give us a little edge.

TRUMP CARD

I told Envil that I was glad we were going to take the ferry. I had regretted the fact that we initially changed our minds. My husband was staring at me the whole time. He knew that none of what I was saying was true, but he is the type of person who will not contradict someone in public unless he just has to. He does not like to argue or be embarrassed, so I used this to my advantage. I continued to tell Envil that I had to go back into the house to use the bathroom and the phone. Not letting Envil know that I never called last night, I definitely wanted the family to know where we were and what was going on. I told Envil that I had talked to the family and I needed to let them know that we were not leaving right away. Our car broke down and we were going to take the ferry ride.

As I had hoped, this sparked some alertness especially in Envil. I could tell because his eyebrows rose quickly when I talked about letting the family know what was going on. He tried to act as though it didn't bother him by saying that would be a good idea. Then I said what Millie said last night, *It's always good to let the family know.* I smirked as I turned to go toward the house.

Next Plan

───◆───

When I turned around, Papa Joe was standing directly behind me. I jumped. *Oh, sorry,* I said. *I didn't know you were that close.*

"Phone don't work," he said in a short and crisp tone.

But it was working last night, I replied.

"Not working now," he insisted.

Wow, I responded. I turned and looked at my husband. From the look on his face, I think he was finally getting the message. *Okay then. I still have to go to the bathroom, but I'll be right back.* I replied.

Millie followed me in the house. As I walked past the check-in counter, I noticed a cigarette lighter on top. I wanted to pick it up without Millie or anyone else noticing me. It was difficult to tell where they were all the time. I desperately needed to collect some items I could conceal and use to defend myself.

While in the bathroom, I took a small can of spray deodorant and hid it in my pocket. After I came out, I asked Millie if she had an ink pen I could use. She said yes and went behind the counter to get one. I quickly grabbed the lighter while her back was turned. She gave me the pen and I wrote a note to my husband. I noticed she was looking back and forth like she suspected something was missing but couldn't quite tell what. To take her mind off the lighter, I asked if the phones went out often here. She looked at me and said, "Huh?"

I said, *The phones, do they go out often?*

"Oh sometimes," she replied.

On the Way to the River

We walked back outside. My husband and Envil were waiting for us on a horse and buggy. "Come on," Envil yelled. "I thought you two got lost. We take the visitors to the water by buggy because it's a little too far to walk unless you just want to. I figured you guys were in a hurry to get home so I pulled it out." Millie and I hopped in.

Envil gave the family history as we went along a dirt path through some trees. I silently passed the note to my husband asking him what he thought now. He nodded his head and patted under his left shoulder. I knew this meant that he had his gun on. I was hoping he had it with him. I felt much safer, but I knew we were not in the clear yet.

AT THE RIVER

Once at the river, there stood a remarkably well-preserved ferryboat. It looked as if it was brand new. I told Envil that his family really did a great job of maintaining everything. Everything was just as beautiful today as they must have been when they were first built, if not better. I constantly tried to soften them even though I felt that their minds were set on harming us.

I believed that they knew I was on to them and in their heads the only way to deal with us was to get rid of us. If they killed the young lady and her son, then most likely they have killed others. At this point in time, there was no room to underestimate what they might do.

Entering the Ferry

―――∾∾―――

As we began to enter the ferry, my chest felt warm again. In the daytime, it is difficult to see the medallion glow. But now I understood why the lady told me that I had to wear it and what she meant when she said that it would protect me. Every time something strange was about to happen, it will forewarn me by getting warm. And sure enough, this time was no different.

On the boat were the aunt and the other sister. Envil said, "I hope ya'll don't mind Aunt T and Ceda coming along with us. I'll be the one driving, and they will keep ya'll company." I just smiled. My husband said the more the merrier. I just hoped he had enough bullets.

Inside the Ferry

When we went to the area where we were to sit, I saw a piece of material caught on the hinge of one of the chairs. It was white and yellow. It looked like the trimming of the missing girl's dress. I dropped my purse so that I could pick it and my purse up at the same time. When I looked at it, I was certain it was from the girl's dress. Suddenly I began to feel very dizzy. The medallion was getting hotter. I couldn't take it off because I did not want the family to see it. So I closed my hand tightly to hold on to the material as the heat from the medallion caused me to faint.

With one hand closed and the other covering my closed hand, I clutched my chest as I began to collapse. My husband grabbed me to keep me from falling down. I could hear him asking me if I was all right, but I could not answer. I could hear Ceda say, "This is going to be easy, T, real easy." I knew they had something sinister in mind, and so did my husband. He never turned his back on them.

THE VISION

While in a daze, I looked at Aunt T and Ceda. They were dressed different than when we first entered the ferry. Both of them were sitting down and not looking at me. There were two other people sitting in between them, the missing lady and her son. Envil was steering the boat. Aunt T kept saying, "Nice son, very nice son," with her same crazy stare and grin. Ceda kept rocking and giggling.

Suddenly Ceda pulled out a club and hit the lady over the head. Her son screamed, but Aunt T held him in place. She told the boy, "You're my son now. Dump her over so the gators can get her!"

Envil hollered, "Wait, I want to get something."

He ran down with a pair of pliers and removed her gold tooth. "Okay," he says, "you can throw her over now. I just would hate to let this good gold tooth drown. Plus, I can use it for myself." As Ceda was trying to toss the body, the hem of the dress snagged on the chair. Envil yanked the dress off and together they threw her over. The noise of the body hitting water brought me back to reality. Ceda and Aunt T were leaning forward looking at me, both of them looking very anxious. I could hear my husband telling them to leave me alone. He had the situation under control.

Getting off the Ferry

W hen he noticed that I was coming around, he asked me if I was okay. I said no and that I wanted to leave right now. Though dizzy, I jumped up and ran as quickly as I could to the carriage, my husband running directly behind me. "What's going on?" Envil yelled. He and his family chased after us. My husband turned and waved his gun. "Get back," he yelled. "I don't want to hurt anyone." He and I climbed into the buggy and headed back to the cottage.

When we were far enough away from the family, I told my husband I was glad he had followed my lead. I explained how the medallion had a really hot feeling that caused me to pass out. While out, I had a vision of what happened to the lady and her son. I also told him how Envil took her tooth and put it in his mouth. I said that I believe that his aunt was right and that Envil, Jake, Ceda and Millie's biological mother is Aunt T. In my vision, Aunt T was obsessed with the lad. I guess she never got over the fact that her children were raised by another woman. She probably tried to replace her kids with someone else's. But it never worked out, so they eventually kill them.

BACK AT THE HOUSE

s we entered back to where the house was, we saw Jake driving our car and the father directing him toward the back of the house. They were most likely going to dump it in the river.

My husband sent up a warning shot and said, "Put your hands up Papa Joe! Get out, Jake! I can see that there is nothing wrong with the car, so we will be taking it now. We don't want any trouble, so keep your hands where we can see them." I tried to grab the can of spray but dropped it from being so anxious.

Papa Joe said, "Where's my family?"

"Safe at the river," my husband replied. "If you want to be safe too, you won't try anything funny. Believe me because I do know how to use this."

We hurried to the car and checked the trunk. Our luggage was still there. To my surprise but pleasure, my husband asked me to drive. He said he wanted to keep his eyes on them. I drove off as fast as possible. My husband was hanging out of the window with the gun pointing at them until we were well out of sight.

THE SHERIFF RETURNS

Once we reached the main highway intersection, we ran into the sheriff. I blew the horn to get his attention. He stopped, and we told him what we experienced as well as what we thought happened to the missing lady and her son. We told him that this family might be responsible for other missing people. I gave him the piece of hem. He took our statements, thanked us, and flew down the small road with his sirens blazing.

My husband began to drive from that point forward. He said that he was glad I kept my first beliefs about the family and that he would try not to take what I said for granted anymore. I told him that it was strange the way the sheriff did not ask our personal information just in case he needed to contact us. My husband thought that maybe he would reach us through his aunt. I felt a little funny but sighed because I was relieved that we were out of there.

CALLED THE AUNT

Then I said, *Oh yes, let me call your aunt and let her know what happened just in case the sheriff contacts her.* When I called, I told her we were back on the main road and I was able to use my cell phone again. I told her that so much happened I forgot to call her from the bed and breakfast. And when I tried to use the phone there, Papa Joe wouldn't let me.

I explained everything and told her that Aunt Julie was on to something in regard to the missing people. I went on and on and explained how lucky we were to run into the sheriff. I also said that he was on his way back to put up some posters and might be contacting her in case he needed more information from us.

She was very quiet. But when she did talk, this is what she said, "Well, we don't have to worry about the sheriff or the rest of the family, and neither do you. The sheriff's daddy had a run-in with us before, and that's why he's missing to this day. So they know not to mess with our family."

I didn't understand what she was talking about. I asked her, *Why would the sheriff try to hurt us? What does that family have to do with the sheriff?*

She said, "The sheriff is the nephew of the owner. If the family is responsible for the missing people, the sheriff is probably the reason why the people are never found. I guess the family thought they would get back at us by messing with ya'll. Good thing you got away safely. Last thing we need here is another feud, because they should know their boundaries."

Conclusion

I dropped the phone in shock of what I heard. The next thing I knew was that my head suddenly jerked forward. I had either fallen asleep or passed out. It was almost dark when I came to and I asked my husband what happened. He said I fell asleep. I asked him if he spoke with his aunt. He said no, not since the last time. I asked if she had told him about the family. "Of course, you were there," he replied. *Oh yeah,* I thought to myself. I figured I just didn't remember from the shock of what I heard.

I then asked my husband how long we had before we would be home. He looked at me and asked me what I was talking about. I said, *What am I talking about? What are you talking about?* As I looked up, I saw the neon sign saying, "Ferry ride next right." My chest was warm. I looked down and the medallion was lit. I then realized that I had been dreaming the whole time. But was it a dream or was it a warning?

I wasn't willing to take any chances, so I began to yell, No, *Kevin.*

Let's not go to the ferry. Let's go back to your aunt's house.

"Stop it," he said. "I'm too tired and we are almost there."

I had to make him listen to me because I feared the worst. With my voice trembling and my body frozen with fright, *No Kevin!* I yelled.

CPSIA information can be obtained
at www.ICGtesting.com
Printed in the USA
FSHW011326260221
78978FS